T0354912

Empires of Dirt

Dennis Mansfield

EMPIRES OF DIRT
BOOK II OF THE TO TRUST IN WHAT WE CANNOT SEE TRILOGY

Book I: To Trust in What We Cannot See is also available at https://dennismansfield.ck.page/products/empires-of-dirt-ebook

iUniverse books may be ordered through booksellers or by contacting:

iUniverse
1663 Liberty Drive
Bloomington, IN 47403
www.iuniverse.com
844-349-9409

For more information visit www.DennisMansfield.com/Author

ISBN: 978-1-6632-6441-1 (sc)
ISBN: 978-1-6632-6442-8 (e)

Library of Congress Control Number: 2024913520

Print information available on the last page.

iUniverse rev. date: 01/03/2025

Dedication

To Cole, Amelia, Eleanor, Dax and Rosie.
The future is yours.

***For more information visit www.
DennisMansfield.com/Author***

"Like anybody, I would like to live a long life. Longevity has its place. But I'm not concerned about that now..."

M.L. King Jr
April 3rd, 1968

"It was more like when a man, after a long sleep, still lying motionless in bed, becomes aware that he is now awake."

C.S. Lewis
Surprised by Joy

"The mind of man makes his plan but God directs his steps."

The Tanakh
Book of Wisdom, 16:9

Section I

The New Story

1

Election Night

Election night was coming to a close. The windy November night seemed to be blowing change across the country

The votes for President had been tallied but not yet announced. Crowds surged, moving forward and sideways, like waves of amber grain, waiting for the announcement of who would lead the United States into the future.

The Republican nominee had years of national experience, a strong career as an officer in the U.S. Navy during wartime, years in elected office in the Senate and a quick and acerbic wit, not particularly handsome but not unpleasant. When asked what would happen if he'd lose this vital race for the Presidency, he quipped, "I'll go home and sleep like a baby...waking up every three hours, crying and screaming." The reporters smiled. They knew it was partially true.

The Democrat nominee was a rare find. A young man of color whose roots mixed in with the roots of the nation. A community organizer, by career, he didn't *really* give speeches, as did other candidates; he *preached* messages. Those messages thrilled his audiences. Throughout the campaign he spoke of "change and hope". And like every good "preacher", when it was time to pass the plate, the donations flowed. As the first black nominee of a major political party, he raised a *lot* of money. He raised even more votes. And he won.

His friend and campaign supporter, Rev. Jesse Jackson, stood in the thick crowd, standing so close to a couple who were waiving small American flags that his image was almost not visible to the television cameras. *Almost.* He knew what was happening. History was happening. And he was crying. Tears flowed and he didn't care. His wet face showed tears of amazement. An African American had just been elected to the Presidency of the United States. Then the announcer's voice interrupted it all, directing all eyes to the stage. "Ladies and gentlemen, it is my great honor to introduce for the first time the, umm, President-elect of the United States." He paused, the crowd could hear a catch in his voice, all stood silently still. He recovered. ".... The President-elect of the United States and his wife, The Reverend M.L. King and our future First Lady Coretta Scott King." Jesse Jackson's tears of joy were America's tears, on the evening of *November 5th, 1968.*

2

Five Years Before

November 22nd, 1963

I'd seen the silent 8mm color motion picture sequence hundreds of times before; in fact, the whole world had.

Yet, somehow it didn't resonate with me how beautiful *that* day actually was, after the early morning rain had faded away and the sun rose. This was one of the most unseasonably warm November days in recent Texas memory; it would provide an ironic backdrop to what would be one of the most chilling, bloody killings ever recorded. The 8mm motion picture sequence broadcast global pain into humanity's soul.

Captured on film by a sportswear clothes manufacturer who originally believed that the morning rain would dampen any images he took, so he initially left his motion picture camera at home.

Later with the sun coming out, Abraham Zapruder was reminded by a co-worker to return to his residence and retrieve his new home-movie camera. He did so and arrived back to a very crowded Dealey Plaza, *just in time*; yet the only vacant spot he could find was atop a cement pedestal. He began filming.

The critically important 8.3 seconds of this 26 second silent film would be replayed and replayed by those in deepest personal sadness, as well as by unattached, clinical research and ballistics analysts; all trying to find out how President Kennedy's assassination had happened. It simply made no sense. A loner killing the President? A conspiracy killing America? Neither case made any sense - not then, not now.

If we were to be successful, our assembled small group of spacetime travelers would ensure that Abraham Zapruder's home movie would, in the *new*-future, only be seen by his kids and grandkids. As Abe might later say to them, "That was the day I saw JFK. A year later he was reelected to the Presidency."

I stood in Dealey Plaza at 11:30 am on November 22nd, 1963 across from where Zapruder would claim his perch, atop the cement pedestal. In one hour, I hoped to see a new history happen directly in front of me. Or more to the point, I planned to see the original *old*-past *not* happen.

Each day since 1898 the Texas Book Depository Building has loomed over the gently sloping streets of Elm Street and Commerce Street. The Dallas pedestrian plaza was often known as the *birthplace* of Dallas; the first home was built there, the first courthouse, too. In fact, the first post office, the first store and the first fraternal lodge were constructed on that gently sloping piece of dirt in the 1840's. Dealey Plaza had always represented life and birth.

The street signs each silently show their names; some of which in the existing spacetime continuum would soon rivet themselves to the collective conscience of the world. Other names, not so, yet all street signs would (unless we were successful) be used to transport the 35th President of the United States to his death. Love Field, Mockingbird Lane, Lemmon Avenue, Turtle Creek Blvd eventually veering to the right and becoming Cedar Springs Road. A left turn at Harwood Street a right turn on Main, a long journey to Houston Street where the shadow of the Old Red

Museum of Dallas County provides noon-day shade for those resting in Dealey Plaza. Houston Street lasts two short blocks until a left is taken onto Elm Street. From that final intersection it's only a measurement of yards, sloping down, down into eternity.

Although built to display *birth*, Dealey Plaza would soon represent *death* – the grisly public death of a vibrant and youthful United States President. John F. Kennedy, 46, the youngest man elected to the U.S. Presidency; and unless history was changed, the youngest President to die in office. But he didn't have to. Not this time.

My spacetime travelling associates and I were committed to altering history in 1963 just as some of us had recently done, fifty short years ago, *last week*, in 1913. There were now eight of us, each with our own responsibility – Dr. Russell Gersema, Louise Abraham, Ernst "Putzi" Hanfstaengl, John Hay, C. S. Lewis, brothers Rick and Zack Besso and me, Will Clark.

We surveyed the plaza. Each walked to his or her station; we knew what to do. We'd planned it months ago, *earlier that week.* I found it oddly comforting that as we'd recently been eyewitnesses in 1913 to the brutal, *yet needful* deaths of Hitler, Stalin, Lenin, Trotsky and Tito in Vienna, we could harness the same science of spacetime travel to *save the lives* of specific key leaders; all of whom had *needlessly* been killed. Men who, as U.S. Presidents, could and would change history – if they were only allowed to live. John F. Kennedy would not die today.

3

A Simple Matter of Timing

November 22nd, 1963

My own Bell and Howell camera in hand, I took my place positioned below, across Elm Street and directly across from 'the grassy knoll', parallel to the concrete pedestal, upon which Abraham Zapruder soon would be standing, his camera in hand. Jack Lewis and Zack Besso joined me there.

I positioned myself to capture all images as the motorcade passed by, with President and Mrs. Kennedy, hopefully unharmed, in it.

Dr. Russell Gersema and John Hay took their positions near the corner of Houston and Main streets, across from each other in clear sight of the Secret Service attachment in the follow up vehicle. Doc had a collapsed white umbrella tucked under his right arm. This was the corner that would see the presidential limo turn right and slowly approach the Texas Book Depository building. Doc stood at the ready, as the Secret Service limo, following the President and Mrs. Kennedy, made its wide righthand turn onto petit Houston, Doc's job was simple; to jump into the street, point his outstretched folded umbrella at the open 6th floor window. His script was simple; "*A sniper, a sniper* – look up, there in the window on the 6th floor. *Police, police*!".

John Hay was further up the short block on Houston St. with a crystal-clear view of the sniper's nest. He carried a TOA Electric Microphone at the ready, to his side. He would then immediately raise it to his lips and keep repeating, "*Sniper at the 6th floor window. Commence firing.*"

Louise Abraham's role was to wait in the 2nd floor breakroom of the Depository building. Hidden in her purse was a snub-nosed Smith & Wesson Victory Model .38 special revolver. Her job was simple. If needed, she would draw that handgun on Lee Harvey Oswald, should he escape the 6th Floor sniper's nest and make his way down to the breakroom. If the Secret Service failed to draw their handguns, as well as the lone AR15 aboard the Secret Service limo, and *if* the local police failed to draw their weapons, Oswald surely would begin his historical escape. She was ready to meet him in the breakroom and disable him with rounds to his legs or knees.

Ernst "Putzi' Hanfstaengl and Rick Besso would be on the roof of the Records Building with a second Mannlicher-Carcano rifle, identical to Oswald's rifle; and a .38 caliber regulation police revolver. After the warning from Doc and John below, Putzi's goal was to take out Lee Harvey Oswald by a double-tap headshot with the police revolver, regardless of whether the Secret Service and the Dallas PD were slow to initiate response. Rick Besso's goal with the second Mannlicher-Carcano was to take scoped aim at any Secret Service member who attempted to grab the lone AR 15 in the Secret Service Detail limo. Rick knew his efforts were just insurance due to Colin McLaren's book, *The Smoking Gun*, in which the author said that a Secret Service Agent accidentally killed JFK when the rifle firing started. There would be *no* possible chance for a mortal error by the Secret Service on *this* November 22nd, 1963. President Kennedy would survive this firefight, no matter what. From above *and* behind himself.

C. S. "Jack" Lewis and Zack Besso each had the same job. And it would only be necessary in the event of a complete failure by the other members which allowed the Presidential motorcade to continue down Elm St. past the concrete colonnade, upon which stood Abraham Zapruder. Lewis and Besso would leap from the curb where we were standing and Jack throw his young body over that of the 46-year-old President of the United States, absorbing any rounds fired, laying down his own life. Zack would throw his even younger body over the First Lady to protect her. Though Zack had many years to live, he was willing to lay his own life down, too.

We all hoped that it would not come to our friends sacrificing themselves, yet we knew that November 22nd 1963 was *already* the day that one of the two men, *C. S. "Jack"* Lewis, would indeed die, at least the one version of him would die. There was nothing he could do in spacetime travel to stop an illness from ending his life. Stopping an assassin, yes. Ending kidney failure, no.

Young Jack Lewis demanded his role.

He scolded us earlier that morning in his Irish accent, "I have to do this. An older version of me will be with the Lord, an hour before President Kennedy dies. Jack Lewis of the present can do something to help John F. Kennedy live for the future" He paused, "Why should President Kennedy have to die, too? No, I won't let that happen."

For a split second the Biblical phrase creased across my mind, 'There's no greater love than this, that a man lay down his life for another.'

23 years earlier, a younger Jack Lewis in The Problem of Pain, had written "God whispers to us in our pleasures, speaks in our conscience, but shouts in our pain. It is His megaphone to rouse a deaf world." Lewis heard God clearly on November 22nd, 1963.

The minutes moved on; our schedule was tied to those minutes. Jack Lewis and I could overhear the motorcycle policemen's radios. Air Force One had landed. The President and Mrs. Kennedy were working the rope line. Then word came that the motorcade was leaving Love Field. My mind raced back to the list of inconsequential street names. We had 37 minutes.

11:50 am the slow-moving motorcade was leaving Love Field to Mockingbird Lane, Lemmon Avenue to Turtle Creek Blvd, then to Cedar Springs Road. On and on to where the shadow of the Old Red Museum of Dallas County provides noon-day shade for those resting in Dealey Plaza. Finally, at 12:27 the slow-moving presidential motorcade took a right on Houston St. just past that noonday sun's shadow and possibly into a new history.

It unfolded right before our eyes.

On cue, Doc and John Hay stepped from their respective curbs along Houston St. and began delivering their lines, yelling, pointing up at the sniper's nest in the 6th Floor of the Texas Book Depository window. Combined with the chaos of the Dallas PD's shrill motorcycle sirens, sounds from Hay's electric megaphone suddenly and painfully roused a deaf world.

The cacophony of sound, motion and action on the curb made the response by the Secret Service accelerate rapidly. Presidential Agents drew their handguns; yet, rounds had not yet been discharged as they seemed to be seeking direction from superiors. Valuable milli-seconds ticked off. All eyes in the crowd were now looking directly at the open window on the corner of the 6th floor of the Texas Book Depository Building. The sniper's face and upper torso were clearly visible. *"Commence firing,"* came the command over a megaphone.

Sweating profusely, Lee Oswald had just swung his 6.55 mm Mannlicher-Carcano rifle from its former original perch to shoot Kennedy in the back of the head, facing down Elm St. to *now* pointing directly up at the motorcade on Houston St., straight into the face of the President of the United States. Putzi had Oswald in his sights; he squeezed off two rounds to Oswald's head, just as a chorus of other rounds from the ground level joined it.

Journalists don't agree on *who* actually fired the first round at the assassin from the motorcade, but they all seemed to agree on who ordered it. Bill Decker certainly took the credit for it. It was reported by the media, Dallas County Sheriff J. E. "Bill" Decker shouted," Commence firing". He supposedly did so from the back seat of the lead vehicle. But that's the media – they have to have somebody, *anybody*, be responsible.

Decker was the same lawman who helped direct another firefight 29-years before, on May 23, 1934 – when, based on his plan, law enforcement officers unleased an equally powerful chorus of rounds and killed notorious murderers Bonnie Parker and Clyde Barrow. Today he was in the middle of an attempted Presidential ambush. It actually wasn't Decker who shouted with an amplified voice in Dallas. God shouted through his own megaphone of pain and the assassin felt it.

The President's Secret Service detail head, Agent Clint Hill, climbed over the back of the Lincoln limousine and covered the Kennedys with his body. Governor Connally and his wife crouched together and leaned into this protective scrum of other secret service agents.

The Presidential motorcade took an immediate and frantic left onto Elm St. in front of the Texas Book Depository Building and raced to the Stemmons Freeway on-ramp, passing Jack Lewis, Zack Besso and me. My Bell and Howell played dueling cameras with the Zapruder camera directly across from us. He would never be known outside of his family; his 26 seconds of film eventually becoming of little interest to even himself – except for capturing a sunny November day in Dallas in 1963 as the President's car sped by, after an assassination attempt.

And C.S. Lewis did not have to lay his life down for another. Nor did Zack Besso.

Both the 5th Floor and the 6th Floor received hundreds of rounds from the motorcade as it made that quick left turn onto Elm Street. Later it was determined that three innocent eyewitnesses, Bonnie Ray Williams, Harold Norman and James Jarman, Jr. who were leaning out of windows to view the motorcade, one floor below the sniper, were all killed by the fusillade of law enforcement gunfire, killing the sniper as well. A lone woman standing at the base of the building, was fatally shot. Midge Galloway was a 22-year-old librarian at the Dallas Central Library. She'd come to see a friend who was supposed to meet her on the sidelines of the motorcade. They'd all be dead, but the President of the United States would still be alive.

Later that night during an evening press conference, law enforcement officers and members of the coroner's office reviewed their examination of the bullet-riddled body of 24-year-old former U.S. Marine Lee Oswald. The coroner announced to the media that Oswald had 44 bullet holes in his body, two were clean head shots by a regulation handgun. Sheriff "Bill" Decker was *obviously* in attendance. People still remember Decker's response when he spoke to the press about the exact number of rounds in Oswald's body.

He chuckled and said matter-of-factly into the microphones bundled on top of the podium, "Well, that's one more bullet hole than we put in Bonnie and Clyde..."

Weeks later, in the investigation, it appeared that Lee Oswald may have squeezed off a single round from the Mannlicher Carcano's muzzle. No one was injured by "Oswald's shot", but the Secret Service's new and somewhat experimental Colt (ArmaLite Rifle) – the AR15 - received a round to the upper receiver parts of the weapon and was damaged beyond any use that day. Luckily, the inexperienced new agent who had just grabbed the unlocked weapon from the car's floorboard was not injured. The weapon was later determined as completely irreparable and destroyed.

It was not Oswald who fired the shot. Rick Besso was accurate with his "just in case" rifle shot.

Twelve minutes later, as our group met at a predetermined spot – tucked behind the now-unimportant grassy knoll, John, Doc, Louise, Putzi, Rick, Zack all stood together and made our way to the adjacent telluric current. Jack Lewis withdrew a card with his own signature on it. Next to his autograph was printed "The Kilns, 1938".

We also stepped into the telluric current and were gone for the next planned destination, through space and time.

4

The Way These Things Start

Present day

My name is Will Clark and I am a widower, a man of faith and an accidental author; a person who never set out to have anything published. *At all.* I just wanted to enjoy life, both now and what's to come. In a certain sense, I am a man *for* the future, *not from* it. I learned how to combine the power of telluric currents and DNA and travel through time and space.

It started with tears.

The unexpected death of my wife in the early 2000's, forced me to write about the sadness I experienced. Being a believer in eternity didn't lessen the deep anguish and pain that I experienced from the loss of my wife; it simply made it more real. A national publisher wanted to investigate those emotions in print. The literary advance paid my bills for a year while I recovered.

People die, loss happens, It's not news. It *is,* however, very isolated. Strangers don't really feel *another* stranger's pain. As N.

W. Clerk wrote in his book, *A Grief Observed,* "The death of a loved one is an amputation.". Strangers can't stand to see pain.

Writing about dead loved-ones extracts a similar response, especially *if* the authors like Mr. Clerk or me are unknown to them. His quote is profound, nonetheless. Many of my comments, at the time, were less profound, though, they were equally heart-felt. The problem with pain is that it bonds together the survivors. Mr. Clerk and I are both bound together by our common experiences *and* we both sold about the same number of grief books – not many.

I'd love to have said that my book eventually became a big seller. It didn't. Buyers for big box bookstores didn't care; although close friends and associates were kind in their comments during those dark days. *They* bought books. People who've lost loved ones *also* bought books. Not quite New York Times Best Seller numbers though.

Mr. Clerk's story is a bit different.

Books about sadness do not to sell in large numbers, unless the author, *himself,* later dies and the publisher re-releases a title, such as *A Grief Observed,* under Mr. Clerk's *real* name – *C.S. Lewis.*

That happened, of course, *after* Lewis passed away on November 22nd, 1963.

C. S. "Jack" Lewis was a deeply thoughtful, wonderful man. We all became quite close to Jack. As an author and as a friend, I felt particularly close to him.

No pen names for me. I'm *only* Will Clark; I haven't even acquired an *un*successful pen name, yet. I didn't say I was an *un*successful author, just that I write books and they sell to those who like my work. (Oh, and I *do* like Lewis's works. I soon found out that I wasn't the only one in our spacetime travelling group who enjoyed the author of the Chronicles of Narnia and so much more.)

Even with my modest sales, I continue writing. Nine books in 7 years. This is my tenth. A few loyal readers tell me that the most recent book I wrote was as *mind-bending* to read as it must have been *time-bending* for me to live it. I wrote what I saw, *what I lived.* And it was utterly amazing as an author; I am indeed an *authority* on this subject. People enjoyed *that* book.

You have before you my newest book – the sequel to *that* first, dimensional spacetime travel story. It's not so much a 'Volume II", as it is a continued extension of what happened next to my friends, Dr. Russell Gersema, Louise Abraham, Ernest "Putzi" Hanfstaengl and to me. We saw the deaths of five men in Vienna; *dying long before they could kill millions of innocent men,* women and children in WWII – the tyrants Hitler, Stalin, Lenin, Trotsky and Tito. We faced that adventure, fifty years before the 1963 assassination of President John F. Kennedy. We had to see if the early deaths of tyrants *really* changed the world for the better. It did not.

What, then, if we saved the lives of good leaders?

C. S. "Jack" Lewis, John Hay, Rick and Zack Besso joined our team to do just that.

But how did we first form *our* team?

5

Joining with C. S. Lewis

1913 Vienna

All of us tend to think that our time on this earth – and *all* the things that are meaningful to us – are somehow meaningful to all others. Space and time do not allow that; spacetime, itself won't be hemmed in by our prejudices, likes or dislikes. While C.S. Lewis's writings meant much to Doc and me, his work meant little or nothing to our other spacetime friends in 1913, as we were tucked inside Doc's library, within his flat in Vienna.

I turned toward them and said, "Jack Lewis was a *most* remarkable thinker, and author in the 20th Century," hoping that Doc would second the idea to join our group, since Lewis was initially his suggestion.

Doc remained silent, watching the others.

Putzi reacted to me, in a mocking tone "*Jack?* I thought you said his name was 'Siesta' Lewis?" Though Doc had not responded, at this point he simply smirked.

I responded to Putzi's silly statement with a semi-stinging rebuke, as someone would do if family members were insulted. "Clive Staples – C. S. – Lewis," I said loudly, as if the increase in volume would make Putzi suddenly understand the greatness of Lewis.

Any silence that follows an emotional outburst is often more powerful than the outburst itself.

Putzi knew this. He looked away and lit another cigarette and forcefully exhaled smoke as he let the silence linger. Then he said, "Alright, alright, C.S. – C.S. Lewis," then he paused as if to consider the foolishness of me even caring about how an unknown writer's name meant anything to me at that point.

As if to put a sharper edge on what he apparently saw as a tedious discussion, in which we were now engaged - about letters and names - he simply asked me, "Why'd you name him *Jack?*"

"I didn't *name* him *Jack*. He named himself *Jack*. It's a name he gave to himself when he was a young boy, after the death of his little dog Jacksie," I paused, trying to remember further specifics. "The little dog was run over by a cart or a horse or something. Young Lewis apparently loved that dog and told his family what his own new name would be Jack." I paused, then continued, "Taking an animal's name for himself seems quite indicative of what he would later write."

Putzi looked at me and deadpanned, "So, to stop a presidential assassin, we're thinking about going to the future to meet an author who, as a little boy, took on the name of a…little dead doggie… and grew up to write… what?" he said, lifting himself off the over-stuffed couch on which he had been sitting throughout this discussion.

Doc took over, "Fantasy books…"

Louise said, "What?"

Doc repeated, "Along with many serious medieval works and academic tomes, he wrote fantasy books about animals that had names and could talk, and demons that wrote letters and… for *our* specific purposes, he wrote about spacetime travel in his Space Trilogy."

Putzi immediately *and* ingloriously flopped back onto the couch, with no words exiting his mouth; just noises – animal-like noises – exiting alongside his cigarette smoke contrails. He seemed most frustrated as we *now* gravitated toward fantasy. Louise joined him in looking deeply puzzled.

Doc continued, "As I said… Mr. Lewis wrote medieval tales of chivalry and much more; he was a friend and colleague of JRR Tolkien." He paused, turned toward his bookshelf and pointed to his section of theology and history books, just above his collection of signed books by M.L. King, John Hay, and others. "Take a look. I have a number of Lewis's signed books on my bookshelf" he said, pointing to the shelf just behind the two over-stuffed chairs. "I find his writing stimulating – he's a man of magic and wonderment." He paused and then said, "Facing the terrible world of a post-Hitler world of Ernest Rohm, we might all find some solace in his writing."

"Or *in him joining us?*" I added.

Doc nodded.

Putzi stood again, this time he looked fascinated, though still a bit confused, by the serious discussion of asking a "fantasy writer" to join us. He sidled over to the book shelf and started glancing at general titles and occasionally pulling down books by various writers and authors. He eventually saw the C.S. Lewis titles but stopped suddenly. Putzi pulled off two books from the shelf written by another author entitled "Where Do We Go From Here?" and "I Have A Dream"; he interrupted the conversation. "When did Martin Luther take on a third name?"

"What do you mean?" I asked.

Putzi responded, "Martin Luther… King…and a Jr, at that? What is this all about? The proud heritage of Germany includes Martin Luther, but nothing about him taking on the last name King. Why not? Is this another response in this spacetime dimension to the things we have done?"

Doc responded, "No, Putzi, they're two different people – actually three different people, when you consider M.L. King's father… who is the Sr."

"We'll talk about him in a bit, if you'd like," Doc said.

"Yes, I would like that," Putzi replied, continued holding the two M.L. King books as he regained his seat.

Louise brought us back on point, "Where is Jack Lewis today? Can we use his current talents? Is that what you both are suggesting?"

Doc took the lead, "No, no, today in 1913 Jack's too young. He's not yet old enough for us to invite him in; this future-author is about to turn 15. His time has not yet arrived for the world to know anything about this future brilliant student, wounded World War I soldier, Oxford scholar and professor."

Again, it was Dr. Russell Gersema holding court, teaching his willing students. I was one of them, enjoying each new bit of trivia, though *I thought* I knew a lot about C.S. Lewis. Yet, I was in error. Doc walked over to the shelf where Putzi had been standing, reached for Lewis's signed copy of *Surprised by Joy*, an autobiography written and autographed in 1955, Doc also reached for his signed 1938 copy of Lewis's spacetime book, *Out of the Silent Planet.*

Doc tucked both books under his left arm and addressed us. "In 1913 Jack Lewis was simply an Irish boy, a Grade 9 student, about to embrace atheism, preparing to leave The Church of Ireland due to deep losses in his life. He was a student at Chartres Preparatory School in the spa-town of Malvern, Worcestershire."

He placed his copy of *Out of the Silent Planet* on the nearby coffee table and then opened the autobiography, *Surprised by Joy.* Putzi nestled deeper into his comfy chair. Louise sat relaxed near the fireplace.

"Surprised by Joy – impatient as the wind. By Wordsworth", Doc read out loud to us. *"The two families from which I spring were as different in temperament as in origin. My father's people were true Welshmen, sentimental, passionate, and rhetorical, easily moved both to anger and to tenderness; men who laughed and cried a great deal and who had not much of talent for happiness. The (other side) were a cooler race. Their minds were critical and ironic and they had the talent for happiness in a high degree – went straight for it as experienced travelers go for the best seat in a train."*

During the late afternoon I relieved Doc in the reading. Louise interrupted a few times with questions. She had a voracious desire for learning. Nothing escaped her attention, nor her memory.

We listened intently. As the late afternoon advanced, Doc continued reading the autobiography of Jack Lewis's life from 1898 to 1931 – the story ending abruptly, *long before* November of 1963 when C.S. Lewis passed into eternity, also ended late in our evening.

Lewis's clarity of writing and logic of mind again pointed towards travelling signposts. We "experienced travelers" were seated indeed in the best seats next to him.

One question in particular, near the end of the book, seemed needful to Louise. I closed the book and listened to her.

"Please read that again, will you, beginning with 'I know very well'." she said.

I re-found the place to which she was referring and began to read.

"I know very well when, but hardly how, the final step was taken. I was driven to Whipsnade one sunny morning. When we set out, I did not believe that Jesus Christ is the Son of God, and when we reached the zoo I did. Yet I had not exactly spent the journey in thought. Nor in great emotion. Emotional is perhaps the last word we can apply to some of the most important events. It was more like when a man, after a long sleep, still lying motionless in bed, becomes aware that he is now awake."

"Yes, that part," Louise said, louder than I think she intended. "That's the part that doesn't' make sense to me. It's gibberish, it's…" she paused, trying unsuccessfully to find the best fitting word.

Doc started what appeared to be a rescue effort of sorts; he liked Lewis, but he'd just not made up his own mind about Lewis's God and his own potential personal conversion. Making Louise feel awkward was certainly *not* a part of his plan. Though his affection for her had changed recently from one of interest and intimacy, as it had been in Vienna, to more of deep respect for her as a person. She, too, had cooled in her romantic thoughts towards Doc. It was just as good for all of us in the group.

I interrupted them both.

"C. S. Lewis is *describing* what happened to himself. He's not *prescribing* a formula for you both, nor for me, not for Putzi, *nor for anyone else* to copy; not even a rote prayer to be easily *mailed* off to God. He's talking about the mystery of eternity, the uniqueness of God. He's addressing at the end of the book what he began with – his emotional *wild Welshman* of a father, often crying and always fighting; this behavior never well-served young Jack Lewis, though the cooler nature of his mother's side brought happiness to him in a way through which he could experience life eventually as an adult – and as well, through which he could experience faith."

Doc squinted and seemed even to nod his head somewhat. Louise did too.

I continued, without noticing any awkward reaction from my friends, though there could have been, I suppose.

"Happiness wasn't enough. He needed more, but it was the achieving of happiness that ultimately caused Jack to accept the greater good - *joy*. Listen to this," I said as I turned to the last page of *Surprised by Joy* and continued reading.

"But what, in conclusion, of Joy? For that, after all, is what the story has mainly been about. To tell you the truth, the subject has lost nearly all interest for me since I became a Christian. I cannot, indeed, complain, like Wordsworth, that the visionary gleam has passed away."

I paused, looked at the faces of my friends, and then I returned to the book and read more. "*But I now know that the experience, considered as a state of my own mind, had never had the kind of importance I once gave it. It was valuable only as a pointer to something other and outer.*"

I stopped reading.

All sighed; it was the group sound of an exhale.

The fullness of Lewis's words during this cooling late night, lay like heavy warm quilts on each of our laps for a long series of hours, warming us, though not uncomfortably.

Midnight had long ago met us; it was time that we retire to our beds and slip out of *our not so silent* planet.

6

1913 Vienna then 1938 The Kilns

Morning now met us. As we rose from sleep, the previous evening's impact remained upon us all; C. S. Lewis's autobiography demanded somehow that we reach out to the author. We discussed the logical probability that he could provide the moral clarity of determining just whose life we should save in order to change the 20th Century and therefore redirect it towards a global community of *life*. Possibly, he could even join us.

First, we had to meet him. Second, we had to convince him of the reality of spacetime travel. Third, we had to either invite him to join us or gain from him who it was he strategically thought we should rescue from premature death for a global benefit.

Sipping on his morning coffee, Doc walked over to the small table upon which he had previously laid Lewis's other book, *Out of the Silent Planet,* and picked it up.

"Well, my friends, in 1938 Lewis published this book," Doc said as he turned to the page directly preceding Chapter 1.

He continued, "Lewis's comment was straight forward, '*Certain slighting references to earlier stories of this type which will be found in the following pages have been put there for purely dramatic purposes. The author would be sorry if any reader supposed he was too stupid to have enjoyed Mr. H. G. Wells' fantasies or too ungrateful to acknowledge his debt to them.*'"

Doc looked at us and said, "Right under this homage to Wells, written in pen is this: '*To the timeless E. Custer. As ever, C. S. Lewis, The Kilns, 1931.*'"

I interrupted him, "Doc… E. Custer? And if he autographed it in '31 but hadn't yet published it until '38, how did *that* happen?"

He shrugged and said, "It may be just another person who shared a well-known last name in the early 20th Century. I was never able to determine to whom the autograph was originally given – only that it was an authentic signature by Jack Lewis with a place attached to it. And the difference of the year? I'm just not sure."

Doc continued, "Jack was around 40 when he published *and signed* this book. His intellect and logic were ahead of their time, and… his DNA is now available for us to use as we travel through spacetime to meet him."

Having remained quiet for some time, Louise finally asked, "Was Lewis a better science fiction writer than H.G. Wells?"

"Better? Heavens no! That's not the word to use. The fact that Lewis 'lifted' – and acknowledged such 'borrowing' of Wells' plot points from The Time Machine – was indeed an homage by Lewis of his supine delight in the pure craft of Wells." Doc paused and took a sip of water, "No, Jack wasn't better, he was, instead, *different* than Wells… much different. His worldview was different and his belief in the destiny of man was different. Wells was futuristic, a utopian pessimist. Lewis looked to the past and was *yet* encouraged by man's desire to overcome this 'Hell on Earth.'"

Putzi, who had also been noticeably quiet, but joined Louise when he spoke up, "So why is it specifically that we need to ask help of Lewis – and not go after Wells instead? Aren't we most interested in the future?"

Doc smiled, turned slightly with outstretched arms and pivoted to his left toward the massive bookshelves, like a ringmaster at a circus and, like a ringmaster, said in a melodious voice, "Because, *my dear friends,* this fine collection of autographed books does *not* include a single signed title by Herbert George Wells. *Period.*"

We all laughed.

I added, "Well that's as good a reason as any!"

Doc looked at me and said rather factually, "Will, shall we use the signed copy *of Out of The Silent Planet* and go meet Jack Lewis?"

I responded, "It just may be time to visit him."

I knew from my experience with other autographs, DNA and previous books we would be meeting Lewis at *The Kilns,* the home he bought with his brother (and another) in 1930 and in which he resided till his death in 1963. I couldn't remember specifically the names of who were also rooming at The Kilns in 1938 with him, but I *did* know it was collection of quite interesting individuals – a number of domestic servants, possibly a gardener/chauffeur, a married music teacher, maybe a confectioner, there *was* an invalid, I *do* remember that – and there was a Fellow of Magdalen College, Oxford, and a tutor – Jack Lewis.

I nodded to Doc, Louise and Putzi and walked over to the Telluric current that issued through the front room of Doc's Vienna flat in 1913. This current allowed us to harness the power of time and space travel. Doc joined me with the book open to the signature from 1938, and therefore to the DNA, of Clive Staples Lewis and invited us to all press down upon the small area of the page adjacent the autograph, as we stepped onto the current.

In less than a moment, we exited our world and landed in an upstairs room of a two-story residence - the Kilns - standing against a wall, next to a magnificent wardrobe.

In the center of the room, at a table alone, with paper and pen before him, sat a 40-ish version of Jack Lewis, puffing on a pipe. Suddenly turning, he stared oddly at the four of us, not scared – just curious.

I was compelled to introduce ourselves; I simply could not resist. I stepped slightly in front of the other three who remained against the wall, next to the wardrobe; I looked at "Jack" Lewis and said quite intentionally, *"Once there were four travelers whose names were Ann, Martin, Rose, and Peter. This story is about something that happened to them…"*

I suppose it was quite eventful to him how I introduced the four of us the way I did. I've always felt that it pays huge dividends to memorize trivia. The four names were the original names of the children in Jack's first-blush idea of a childhood book about witches, a lion and talking animals. The book would take ten more years, including a second world war and therefore many war orphans staying at The Kilns with Lewis, his brother, Warnie, and other assorted tenants, to allow Peter, Susan, Edmund, and Lucy eventual entrance into Narnia.

But this was still 1938 and his large wooden wardrobe only had clothes in it.

"Ann, Martin, Rose, and Peter?" he said with a type of unexpected shriek, pointing down at the sheet of paper on which he had just seconds prior to our arrival written those exact names, having just scratched with his fountain pen the final *r* in the then-youngest character's name, *Peter.*

Jack Lewis was as much surprised at my introduction, using those specific names, as he was at the very magical appearance of us in his upper room, next to his magnificent wardrobe. And that's how we were able to catch *and keep* the attention of C. S. Lewis.

7

Truth Never Fears Investigation

1938 The Kilns

We stayed for several hours. We could not leave and he did not want us to.

Once the entire story was told to Jack, he grasped the full impact of what it was we desired of him. The deepest pain, upon his request, was explaining that we knew his date with eternity – and how kidney failure would be his cause of death, just one week shy of his 65th birthday.

Ever the pragmatic analyst and academic, Jack Lewis accepted the reality.

Had he wanted, he could have simply provided his take on which of the key American Presidents must be saved, and then go on to live out his life in academia, for 25 more years.

But he did not do that. Instead, his request was to join us as we traveled forward and backward.

He suggested that Abraham Lincoln's life must be spared and even logically suggested how doing so would alter the balance of international power, by eliminating, as he put it, "the succession of fools" who became President from 1865 to 1932. He understood the politics of ascension in ancient medieval history and saw that he might just be able to apply those lessons learned to both the past and near-future of the world.

Doc agreed and explained that in order to return to save Lincoln's life, we would have to pick up an additional two more members, currently living in 1913 in Vienna.

After several hours of discussion and tea, we stood up and moved back to the nearby Telluric current by which we arrived. Doc opened a book to the needed page with DNA from Vienna in 1913. We were returning with a new member. C. S. Lewis, future author of what would become one the finest adventure tales ever told, looked at Doc, Putzi, Louise and me with a smile, placed his hand on top of ours and said, "If ever I remembered my life in this world, it was as one remembers a dream." And we were gone.

8

Rohm's Reich

1913 Vienna

Jack Lewis, Louise Abraham, Putzi Hanfstaengl, Doc Russell Gersema and I arrived in Doc's flat in Vienna. Jack was astounded at the speed and the quiet of traveling by Telluric current.

"I've got to capture this form of travel in my writing of those four children about whom I will be writing. It's utterly marvelous," Jack said. "They could travel by Telluric current!"

I looked at Doc with a side glance and then mentioned quietly, "Well, that's possible, but it sure would be nice to take something scary from childhood and turn it into a portal to a new world."

Jack lit up his pipe and responded, "Quite possibly. I could have them depart through a loo."

I looked at Putzi, not understanding what the word meant, and he responded with a toilet flushing motion."

"Eww, I responded, no, no that won't work… how about a wardro…"

Doc interrupted me.

It was now Doc's time to explain to our growing band of adventurers what it was that we were now facing. Our discussion took several hours to bring everyone up-to-date on what *is going to* happen in the new alt-history from 1913 through Ernst Rohm's death in the late 1980's.

Doc initiated that discussion, "Rohm's more brutal than Hitler could ever have been, had *Der Fuhrer* lived."

Putzi reacted, "My God, that's saying something."

I added, "Rohm was somehow able to stop World War I from happening and create a false peace - through terrorist acts of murder and eventually, genocide. They called it the Great Peace. How ironic… and he turned the world into a series of Fascist states and nations."

The others in our group appeared deeply affected by the "alternative world" we would now be encountering. "It would be a hellish world in *this* time and space". I continued. "The way Rohm developed a group of commando terrorists that simultaneously attacked America, France, and England, using mustard gas to incapacitate so many in each nation's capital, is devilishly terrible: three combined strikes, three weak governments unable to match his combined Central European armies, two dead prime ministers, and one dead U.S. President.

After that, Rohm broke the will of each nation and built several death camps throughout the defeated countries It was almost supernatural." I corrected myself, "It WAS supernatural. Rohm's fascination with spiritualism of the early 20th century was bizarre. He called on beings from another dimension to visit Earth. He was a huge proponent regarding the existence of extraterrestrial beings from other galaxies."

Jack asked, "He believes, as H.G. Wells does, that spacemen are real?"

Doc responded, "Yes, in fact, Rohm was a contemporary of America's General Douglas MacArthur. Both men anticipated warfare would come from outside the star system. MacArthur told the Corps of Cadets at West Point, 'We speak…of ultimate conflict between a united human race and the sinister forces of some other planetary galaxy.'

MacArthur cautioned against it. Rohm welcomed it."

We all sat in Doc's library, silently considering what, if anything, we could all do to again change history; this time for the better.

"This isn't about Hitler anymore; it's doubly worse than what *that* monster delivered," I said.

Deep in thought, Doc responded, "The events of impacting alternative history clearly show that killing even the evilest Nazi, does not kill evil."

Doc stared up and out, as if he was no longer with us. "If we are going to save Lincoln's life we'll need to think differently. We turned our eyes toward him. He continued slowly, "I think we need to go deeper into history and prove that wars, like the Panthay Rebellion (and more importantly the Dungan Revolt) in China, from the mid-1850's to the mid-1870's add a huge impact on the culture of national killing. Almost 21 million people died in China during that time by swords, spears and hand-to-hand killing – way before firearms. The art of killing spread to Europe. Then, during the 1860's in North America, the U.S. Civil War triggered what would a century later be called the military-industrial complex of mechanized mass death from cannonade, rifle and pistol – on the battlefield and off. The magnitude of death during the American Civil War was increased by the escalation and invention of weaponry. Ultimately, within four score years after the Civil War, the world had atomic bombs – and deployed two of them in wartime. We need to expand our circle; *and* we need to return to America sometime between 1861 and 1865 to slow or stop that escalation process *and* invention progress. We'll need to shorten the Civil War. We'll need more people to help us. Good people. People I can trust."

An uneasy tension in the group began to evidence itself, as Doc spoke.

Realizing this, Doc looked up and with a slight smile in his eyes, he continued "We'll start with the ablest history researchers I know. They're brothers, and spacetime travelers like us; they live right here in the *1913 version of Vienna*." He paused and smiled more broadly, "And man, do they love whiskey, oldies and classic rock!"

9

The Brothers Besso

Vienna 1913

You couldn't find two more different brothers, in *any* spacetime continuum. Ever.

And yet, actually *finding* Rick and Zack Besso in Vienna, Austria in 1913 proved quite easy. Doc was familiar with their flat; he was previously responsible for bringing them through time and space in another adventure a long time ago, to where they had established a new life and a way to travel across the universe. That story's for another time. But today's time was just for us.

"I can't wait to hear this," Louise said, while we all gathered up our coats and headed out the door, following Doc. As we trudged through the snow, bundled-up and excited about what might be just around the corner for us, Doc began to tell us about the Besso Brothers.

"These two men are remarkable," Doc began. "Rick's a West Point Graduate, Class of '78."

"1878?" asked Putzi.

Doc answered, "No, a century later - 1978. Among many other assignments, he served as a military attaché in Paris and throughout Europe – helping ambassadors, protecting their families and staffs. An Airborne Ranger, a tough son of a gun. A real fighter and a strong leader. He served during the future American Gulf Wars, retiring only when age demanded that he pack up his uniforms, medals, memories and move on. He's brilliant in physics. I stumbled across him in a dusty back-alley bar in Tangiers just as he was finishing his Army career. But that, too, is another tale to be told one day."

Doc led us around a large puddle of slushy wintry water that was directly in our path.

"His brother, Zack, is a classic hard-rocker with music who also *loves* history. He's pretty logical, too. Rick and he have a real taste for Dave Pickerell's whisky."

"Dave Pickerell?" I asked.

"Yep, an amazing man of amazing talent. He was in Rick Besso's West Point Class. Pickerell also got a master's degree in chemistry. He oversaw the creation of Kentucky bourbon that turned into… excuse me … *will* turn into a huge business in the 2000's. He even crafted a whiskey for Metallica - partnering with the heavy metal band to create "Blackened," a blend of American whiskeys. They're finished in oak barrels and Metallica's music serenades the whiskey as a sort of 'sonic enhancement'. They always travel with *Blackened…*"

Putzi asked, "Metallica?"

Doc responded, "Hard rock musicians."

Putzi looked utterly confused.

Jack Lewis looked amused. "Seems that language is continuing to change…" he said as he lit his Comoy pipe.

"We'll fill you in later," Doc said in a throw-away sort of fashion. He slowed to a stop and looked at the address on the flat in front of him, "Here it is. Home of the Brothers Besso." He then turned to all of us, smiled and said, "You think spacetime travel was a trip…get ready for these guys."

Doc knocked at the door.

A whole new world opened as Zack Besso met us and waved us in; his long hair, wild and erratic. "Hey Rick, Doc's here with some guests!"

What?" said a man's voice, barely discernable from another room and under the barrage of hard rock music blaring in the background.

Doc turned to Putzi and gestured with a knowing look and an air of introduction by extending his left hand, "Metallica!"

Putzi grimaced.

Turning to where his brother was, Zack yelled again, "Doc's *here* with some guests!"

"Are you kidding me?" Rick Besso ratcheted down the music volume as he rounded the corner into the hallway from the breakfast room with a silly kitchen apron on that said 'Beat Navy' across it, a damp rag in his hands, a high-and-tight military haircut and a smile that crossed his face with ease.

"Doc, it's so good to have you drop by! How long's it been?"

They hugged.

Doc smiled, "Who knows? It's only time…"

Rick and Zack laughed.

Zack gave him a hug, as he continued, "Come on in, we're making pancakes, bacon and eggs – and it'll take very little to multiply the amount of food! Food tastes better when you share it, anyway." Pointing at us, he added "Hi there! Who are you?"

Doc introduced us all by first names only, as we removed our winter coats, hanging them on the hall tree. We all seemed to glide toward the warmth of the kitchen. And the smell of food

"Are you folks hungry?" Zack asked.

Ravenous for breakfast, we gave a corporate *'Yes'*, and settled into the Besso Brothers' kitchen. Rick and Zack had obviously been up early, standing at the coke-burning stove, cooking their morning meal. Smoking his own Comoy pipe, Zack's quick movement inadvertently flicked Gold Block pipe ash onto the pans and plates, pushing glasses and mixing bowls into the large sink. He didn't care, he needed the pans and pots out of the way. He puckered his lips and blew away most of the ash.

Zack asked, "Something huge must be happening, Doc, to have so large a team with you. Have you been studying John Mack's works on alien abductions again?"

"What?" asked Louise, looking as though she was completely lost on this subject.

Rick interrupted, "It's just something that he and my brother always discuss when they get together. They seem to believe that the universe is full of beings seeking to visit Planet Earth and abduct specimens for experimentation, eventually returning them back to the points where they found them. And certainly, don't get them started on the Nephilim and that other guy, Tim Remington, from Coeur d'Alene."

Louise responded, "Who? What?"

Zack shrugged, turned away from his brother and looked directly at Doc, "We'll get to that later...what brings you to us, this morning?"

Rick motioned to us to take a seat in the kitchen.

Each of us settled into our seats around the table. Zack turned from the sink and looked at his friend and ours, awaiting a response from Doc to his brother's question. Jack Lewis seemed to be taking it all in, just listening.

"Well, my two *wild* friends, we're in a dilemma and I think you may be able to help us," Doc responded. "And NO, it's not about Biblical giants, flying saucers or flying discs... at least I don't think it is."

Louise engaged once more, this time with a bit more agitation, "Giants, you mean from the Torah? Saucers and discs that fly?"

Zack responded kindly to Louise, "I'll show you some things later by Dr. John Mack from Harvard Medical School. One day he will be the head of psychiatry and win a Pulitzer Prize as an author."

"What's a Pulitzer Prize?" Louise innocently asked.

Zack responded, "Oh yeah, that's right, you wouldn't know about it. It won't be initiated until 1917 – four years from now."

Jack turned to me, as he blew pipe smoke from the left side of his mouth, "This entire type of conversation is fascinating for me to absorb. Fascinating. Oh, and Zack, nice pipe." He clinched the button in his teeth at the lip of the pipe and refocused himself on the conversation.

Zack smiled, not knowing who it was who had just addressed him *and* who had a penchant for the same type of pipe.

Rick jumped back in. "Again, how big is this new gig?" he asked, as he threw more medium sized blobs of pancake mix onto the hot, black flatware pan, which also had a slab of bacon sizzling on it.

Doc explained what we'd just been through with the murders at Café Central, speaking a sort of spacetime short-hand to the brothers, whose expressions showed they'd shared similar hard experiences in the past with Dr. Russell Gersema. They both nodded at different times, each asking an occasional clarifying question on distinct points of the adventure.

Rick's summary was clear and cogent, "Sir Isaac Newton's blend of scientific brilliance and biblical accuracy points to a date, 2060, apparently ordained by God, the world as we know it will end," he paused. "Am I correct?"

Doc responded, "Well, almost…2060 is just the earliest date it could happen, Newton wrote in 1704."

Rick nodded and then leaned toward Doc, as he sat at the table with us, glanced and nodded at Zack, and then asked his final question of Doc, "Ok…how may we help you?"

"I want you both to join us as we use spacetime travel, to amend history and change the world from Newton's prophesy of global destruction, after 2060." Doc's simple and straight forward request of the brothers surprised me.

No one seemed bothered at all by Doc's comment about amending history or Rick's casual use of the words "ordained by

God". Somehow, the whole ethos seemed to have a supernatural feel to it. The conversation's seriousness invaded the room.

Zack had a different thing in mind. He reached over to his Edison phonograph and increased the volume on R.E.M.'s most appropriate chorus for the moment. He began joining the music, loudly singing, "It's the End of the World as We Know It" and paused just enough to sing the final lyric, "*'And I feel fine'*… so let's eat breakfast."

C.S. Lewis listened to the phonograph's song; a delight blossomed in his eyes.

We laughed out loud. No one needed to ask us a second time to breakfast. After all, the world as we knew it *was* apparently ending.

The meal's conversation went all over the map – from quantum physics and how Doc met the two brothers in the future of the last decade of the 20th century, to what the three of them had previously done during their own spacetime travel adventures. We learned what the Besso Brothers listen to and read: George Orwell, Douglas MacArthur, Aldous Huxley, H. G. Wells and others. Doc spoke about Brian Green's works, including *The Elegant Universe.* I mentioned that I enjoy C. S. Lewis's many books.

Zack responded, "I enjoy C.S. Lewis, too – especially his Space Trilogy – that's what originally connected Rick and me to Doc."

Doc paused.

Jack smiled, again remaining anonymous.

Zack continued, "In fact, I enjoy most of Lewis's works… but what is it with an author using his or her initials?" No one responded, especially not Jack. He smiled, again, though.

Zack continued, "Let's examine the two-volume autobiography by U.S. Grant and go on from there. Afterall, it's the book set that initiated your travels, right, like *C. S.* Lewis's book set initiated our travels?"

Doc nodded again.

Zack added "And... we ought to use U.S. Grant's memoir and travel baek ASAP in spacetime to, among many other far more serious things, ask him why he changed his name to the initials Is that all A-OK?"

We could tell that Zack Besso was loving this verbal banter. "U.S.? I mean, come on, Hiram Ulysses Grant changed his name to the nation's initials!" He paused for effect, "Thank God he didn't choose *Central South America* ... then C.S. Lewis could meet C.S.A. Grant...."

Jack began to laugh. Others only chuckled. Jack didn't care, "I've said this before, but it bears repeating, my happiest hours are spent with three or four old friends in old clothes tramping together and putting up in small pubs – or else sitting up till the small hours in someone's college room talking nonsense, poetry, theology, metaphysics over beer, tea, and pipes. There's no sound I like better than adult male laughter." Then he paused and quickly said to Louise, "No offense intended, Louise."

"None received," she said with a twinkle in her eye.

Zack didn't miss a beat; a few more chuckles surfaced. "Believe it or not, C. S. Lewis said something quite similar to that."

The eyes of *'Ann, Martin, Rose, and Peter'* all looked at Jack.

He responded to Zack, "Well my young liege, I will guarantee that Clive Staples Lewis said exactly those words."

He paused, lit his pipe, just as Zack lit his own exact pipe, and exhaled some delicious scents into the air.

Zack asked, "When?"

Jack answered, "Just now."

10

Breakfast

1913

Zack and Rick realized, good naturedly, that they'd been intentionally and intellectually bush-whacked by Doc and our group. Most importantly by Jack Lewis, himself. After proper full name introduction, they all shook hands.

And they were full of glee, realizing that Lewis, age 40, would be among our group.

We sat enjoying Zack's continued monologue, even as we enjoyed his breakfast meal, he continued pointing at Jack: "C.S. Lewis, M. L. King, J.F. Kennedy, R.F. Kennedy, A. Lincoln" as he paused and flipped some German pancakes and continued, "E. B. White, A. A. Milne, H.G. Wells, T. S. Elliot and the author with the *extra* letter, J.R.R. Tolkien." He paused, holding a huge ladle full of pancake mix and pointed it in the direction of the table.

"Why?" he asked us, moving the ladle from one hand to the other while flipping a hand-towel over his shoulder, he walked over to the Edison phonograph and placed another album on it. "Why the use of the initials?"

Putzi injected, "I don't know *who* many of these people are with the initials – they must eventually become famous after 1913. I mean I *do* know of H.G. Wells and, *of course,* A. Lincoln…"

Jack interrupted, "Wells influenced me greatly in my appreciation of science fiction. Lincoln influenced me by his remarkable prose – almost poetry."

Zack looked at Putzi and Jack; he then slowly at us. "So, you think you two 'know' Lincoln, do you?"

The menacing ladle of wet pancake mix slopped back and forth as he swung it and asked his question of Louise and our group…waiting. "Did you know he's in a Rock n' Roll song?

Putzi sputtered, "Rock n' roll… here we go again. Does Mr. Lincoln know Bingo?"

Jack asked, "What?"

I responded, "Ringo…" and dismissed the comment with the wave of my hand.

Putzi nodded.

Zack added, "I'll bet that Doc told you we party and *only* listen to oldies and classic rock, right?" Not waiting to receive a response, he continued, "Not so! To quote the unappreciated non-theologian and lyrical talent, William Martin Joel:

'It's the next phase, new wave, dance craze, anyways
It's still rock & roll to me.
Everybody's talkin' 'bout the new sound
Funny, but it's still rock and roll to me'"

Putzi shrugged but was suddenly interrupted by a completely different song, initiated by our musical host for the breakfast. Shirley Ellis' 1964 song exploded in our ears like a loud alarm clock. A couple of us jumped like scared cats, especially Putzi and Jack.

Not Zack. He led us in song, with that sloppy ladle becoming a sort of karaoke microphone.

"Lincoln, Lincoln bo-binkin, banana fana fo finkin fee fi mo minkin, Lincoln..."

Zack embraced the lyrics of the song and then yelled above the music, apparently for effect, "And then there's *A. Lincoln.*"

He danced around, then slowly turned down the volume of the song and asked in a very well-modulated voice, "Why just the initial *A*? Why not *Abe* or just simply *Lincoln,* like the song" He didn't pause; he wasn't really seeking an answer. "For most of his life, Lincoln simply used his first initial when he signed papers or speeches. *A. Lincoln.* Even his Springfield law practice's outdoor sign used only his first initial and his last name."

Then Rick added, "What my brother's trying to say is that maybe we should look seriously at the impact of Lincoln's death on the future? You mentioned that you want to see about saving people's lives from pending wars and therefore changing history through that method, right? And your time frame was during 1861 to 1865, right? Is that what you were thinkin' about Lincoln?" He paused, realized what he had just said and then followed it up with, "Man, I'm starting to sound like my brother!"

"We are already ahead of you. Lincoln is already our first choice." Jack Lewis said. Doc nodded. He was doing a lot of nodding, while the Besso Brothers were on a roll.

Zack added, "President Lincoln is mentioned throughout Grant's book. In fact, Grant was supposed to be with Lincoln at Ford's Theater on the evening he was assassinated, wasn't he?"

I joined Doc and we nodded some more.

Rick said, "Indeed, we ought to go see Lincoln..."

Zack said, "Let's make our plan and then use the telluric currents, here in Vienna, to return to a key date and place that would help end the Civil War early, ok?"

Rick shook his head, "I'm game, brudda."

Zack added, "I bet he never autographed anything with 'Bo Binkin Lincoln, did he?"

We all laughed. The sloppy pancake mix was dripping down the ladle/karaoke mic handle onto Zack's arm and elbow as he started to sing again, this time to "Weird Al" Yankovic's "Eat it" version of Michael Jackson's song "Beat It." The smell of the food seemed to round out the effect. The background music transitioned to Weird Al's song.

The lyrics took flight, *"How come you're always such a fussy young man? Don't want no Captain Crunch, don't want no Raisin Bran…"*

Putzi said, "Captain Crunch?"

The lyrics continued, *"So eat, just eat it…"*

Joy was starting to surprise us, even as Zack was leading us on a kind of a wild musical journey. Weird Al continued serenading in the background.

Jack was most surprised by the joy; it only seemed appropriate.

"Get yourself an egg and beat it." The song kept going in the background.

I picked up the original question about initials and said with a loud voice, "Sometimes initials are used because, like you Jack, the owner of the name simply didn't like his or her own birthname, so a choice was made to professionally use their initials, or a shortened name, rather than a pen name." I pointed backward with my thumb at the record and added, "like Weird Al."

Doc laughed as he heard a lyric slip through, *"Have some more chicken, have some more pie, it doesn't matter if it's broiled or fried, just eat it…"*

I continued, "Sometimes it's what others call them – or even how they marketed themselves. In 1860, Abraham Lincoln campaigned under the nickname, "Old Abe" – and he was only 52-years-old. In the future, 1960 America will elect a young 43-year-old John F. Kennedy as President; the campaign motto will be *'All the way with JFK.'* He'd previously never been referred to as JFK, though he *may* have fulfilled the motto a little too often on the campaign trail." Rick's right eyebrow raised as I chuckled.

There was a sight pause. Weird Al added, *"Just eat it, eat it, eat it, don't you make me repeat it…"*

Putzi stuffed the final pancake, into his mouth two additional pieces of bacon and a huge dollop of whipped topping.

Zack and Rick looked on, amazed at the German's capacity to consume vast quantities of food while talking.

Louise began pretending in a faux-German accent that she was Putzi's mother, crowing about her brilliant little son. His eyes began to twinkle, as he looked up from his plate. The know-it-all *wind bag* in him departed – replaced by a breath of fresh air that had taken over – the "little kids" in all of us began to surface. I could see Zack and Rick rolling up their wet towels in tight rat-tails, preparing to *pop* Putzi, if needed.

Louise blurted, "Ja, you were the smartest little kid in Kindergarten!"; she laughed and pinched Putzi's very full cheek! He began chuckling, trying to contain himself.

Pinching the other fuller cheek, Doc joined the fun and added in a high shrill German voice, "Putzi, my Putzi, we love you!"

Suddenly, Putzi's own chuckle became a rumble and for a spit-second, Doc looked at me, both of us remembering how, in Vienna's Café Central, Putzie Hanfstaengl had projectile-christened Mark Twain's brilliantly white suit with dark coffee and pastry stains, in much the same situation.

Doc and I dove for the floor, but it was too late for the rest. Louise sat erect in her seat, Zack and Rick were leaning against the table and the stove. Jack was standing like a statue, disbelieving all he saw.

Weird Al's timing was impeccable, *"Have a banana, have a whole bunch, it doesn't matter what you had for lunch, just eat it…"*

Then, Putzi 'blew'; *this time* for all to see, and before the Brothers Besso could stop the attack with the wet rattails. Putzi had the power of a volcano. The food he previously stuffed into his large mouth, spewed all over us like a bacon/pancake mixed, nonlethal, shrapnel explosion. *None* hurt, but some hit; a few of us were sickened, but not Putzi. He began laughing and slapping the table out of sheer joy and utter messiness. He was once again that chubby little German kid that Mark Twain had previously known – only now we all saw his honest self-deprecating messy humor.

"I am a little piggy but *you* need the bath!" he laughed as he picked up two full water pitchers and quickly doused us.

Zack dropped his wet-towel rattail and grabbed the remaining pancake mix and ladle, and whirled it in the air like a helicopter rotor, splashing any and all victims. Rick, ever the good soldier, shielded himself against his brother and the tall German by grabbing a large carving tray off the counter and holding it in front of his face, lessening the splatter, but attacking with glasses of water or milk. Louise, Doc and I kept laughing, even as we reached for our own water and milk glasses and responded in like action.

It was a spacetime food-fight for the ages.

Taking out a handkerchief to wipe clean his smirched glasses, Jack said, "Making animals speak is nothing compared to making humans contain themselves."

He convulsively laughed out loud and then quickly grabbed a counter top edge for his own stability, amid the wet wreckage.

11

Unpacking a New Reality

The Besso Brothers' flat
1913 Vienna

We ended up slipping and sliding on the floor of the kitchen, grasping for anything that would keep us standing. It didn't work. We slipped on the floor, laughing and howling, wet as can be.

For a time.

Then we became exhausted and simply halted our food hostilities and reached for rags to wipe off the wet food from our faces, shoulders and arms.

Next, we began cleaning the walls, the chairs and the counters. In time the entire room was as clean as the Mess Hall at West Point.

We heaved a final corporate breath of release through our laughter and stood to our feet. We stacked the now-empty, clean dripping plates, glasses and place-settings upon each other in the sink to dry and sat down, once again around the table.

Zack returned to his original question, as if none of the nonsense had happened, and asked Jack directly, "So why do *famous* people use their initials and nicknames – like C.S. Lewis?" He wiped the final slash of pancake/bacon shrapnel from his own face.

A bit worn out from these two brothers and their fun and exhaustive playfulness, I interrupted and blurted out, "Who knows why they all used their initials? Who cares that they did that? *They did it.*"

Jack took the bait and responded, "Truly, who knows why we do that? Indeed, it could be the custom of the times, it could be just a curiosity in literature, I suppose," he added, "And in the end, you might really need to review a handful of them before my time, starting with … A. Lincoln."

"I think Jack is right," Putzi added. "Who cares about the names and initials…America's capital city should be our new focus now."

Jack Lewis looked at Putzi and continued, "*Thank you* to the man who goes by the strangest nickname of all time, 'Putzi'!" He finished wiping pancake batter and sausage parts off of his balding head, using an unfurled white hand-towel.

Putzi laughed, "Ja, but my nickname's not strange in Germany! After all, it means 'little fellow'- and here I am well over six feet four. So, sometimes *odd* names should stick, I suppose, just for the fun of it."

Doc added in, "Not all stick; a writer in the future, Aldous Huxley, was nicknamed Ogie, as a young boy because his brother said he was as strange as an ogre, as a child! He became quite a teller of horrific tales in his time. I have a signed copy of his book, Brave New World, in my library. It's in the common death dates section…"

"The what?' Rick asked as his attention was suddenly redirected like a laser, while he removed and folded his kitchen apron.

Doc responded, "Rick, you know I classify my books in personally useful ways."

Rick said, "Sure, but ... by common death dates?"

Putzi looked curiously at Doc, too. "Who has common death dates? You mean the same day, the same year?"

Doc nodded, "Yep – for example, future U. S. President John F. Kennedy and Aldous "Ogie" Huxley died on the same day, November 22nd 1963."

Then, the reality of what was just said sunk in on Doc, since he also knew that Jack Lewis's date of death was November 22nd, 1963 too. The very same day.

Jack took a quick breath, shot a look at the floor with a quizzical expression and then slowly lifted his face toward Doc, "All my life in this world and all my adventures... have only been the cover and the title page: now at last they... will be... the beginning Chapter One of the Great Story, which no one on earth has read; which goes on forever; in which every chapter is better than the one before, he paused a great long time. "And I will be ready for it." He looked at all of us, "But today is today; and we must be alive and able to be used for others."

Jack retired to a bedroom to rest, for he was greatly exhausted, especially by the reminder of his own death.

Rick, Zack, Putzi, Louise and I sat up, surprised. *How had we <u>not</u> known this fact, I thought.*

Louise added, "The same day of *the same year*?"

Doc responded, "Within hours of each other."

"Jack Lewis, at The Kilns, Jack Kennedy in Dallas, and Aldous Huxley in Los Angeles. All in that order and all within eight hours of each another."

Putzi put away his own wet rag; Louise and I joined him as he leaned forward against the kitchen table

Turning the kitchen table chair around and leaning on the arched wooden back of it, Doc asked, "I think it's important that we know the spacetime impact of the deaths of A. Lincoln... and then Jack Kennedy and Jack Lewis along with some of the others in the world. I'm not sure how I see Huxley fitting into our plan, though."

We nodded.

Rick asked Doc a simple question, "Maybe Putzi has a point about seeking help from Grant and saving the life of President Lincoln during the Civil War. Why don't we first start there and see how we could change things before we head into the future of Kennedy and any others?"

Stradling the kitchen chair, Doc leaned even more toward us, looked at the floor, then looking up at Rick. Doc said, "Saving the lives – rather than taking the lives – of important global historical figures may be exactly *why* we're here. Let's *do* meet with General Grant and President Lincoln. If we can shorten the American Civil War, we may be able to slow the global expansion of war itself. Maybe even end it."

Then he looked at Zack, and chuckled, "But no more spontaneous food fights from you, or World War III might indeed break out, before the flying saucers arrive, got it?'

Louise looked puzzled, "*Wait,* there was a World War I and II – and they involved flying saucers?"

Rick Besso responded with a sardonic chuckle as he straightened his West Point ring with his right thumb against his right ring finger, nodded and said to our sole female member, "Exactly Doc's point, Louise."

Louise responded, "Well, I hadn't laughed that much in a long time… and if this is the way you two wild Besso Brothers operate in spacetime travel, my guess is that we've just begun to laugh."

Zack said, "And from everything I've read about A. Lincoln's humor, we may have to be on guard for *him* making *us* laugh even more!"

Louise added, "Really? For some reason, I've only ever thought of President Lincoln as a somber man. Not as a man of laughter."

Throwing the final wet rag into the Besso Brothers's open hamper, Doc added, "After Jack awakens from his rest, let's head back to my flat. I've also got a signed set of books in my library that will show us Lincoln as he really was – they were written by his personal secretaries, John Hay and John Nicolay."

Rick looked at Zack and directed him with a nod of his head towards the phonograph. On Edison's open-horn record player Zack replaced Weird Al with Willie Nelson. The only song that fit, rang out... *On the Road Again.*

We just didn't know how long on the road of spacetime travel would be, nor did we know whose dark, cold shadow was following us.

1947 had some things of its own ready for the world that might just help us.

Section II

12

Ken Arnold and Unidentified Aerial Phenomena

1947

Looming over us was always the shadow of whoever – or whatever – was around us as we journeyed by spacetime travel. Evil had followed us through space and time. One theory is anchored to the year 1947.

32-year-old Ken Arnold was the first to see flying saucers *and* have news media report it. It was June 25th, 1947 and Arnold, a Boise, Idaho businessman, was flying his own plane between Mount Rainier and Mount Adams when he saw nine saucer-like aircraft flying in formation at an altitude of around 10,000 feet. His comments to the press upon landing in eastern Oregon were that the crafts travelled at about 1,200 miles an hour, an unbelievable speed in 1947.

The article in the East Oregonian that interviewed him was straight forward:

"Ken Arnold was flying from Chehalis, Washington, to Yakima in his single-engine CallAir A-2 when he took a detour around Mount Rainer to look for the wreckage of a Curtis Commando R5C transport plane that crashed Dec. 10, 1946, with 32 Marines aboard. Finding the plane meant a $5,000 reward.

He estimated he was 25-28 miles from Mount Rainier and climbed to 9,200 feet and saw to his left a chain of objects, he said, that looked like the "tail of a Chinese kite."

Arnold considered they could be geese, but they were flying south in summer and too high. He wrote off new jet planes because "their motion was wrong for jet jobs." He opened his window in case they were reflections and still saw the objects.

Arnold said they were as "big as a four-engine airplane" and "flat like a pie-pan, and somewhat bat-shaped" and flashed bright enough to temporarily blind him. They were "saucer-like" he said, and moved "like a fish flipping in the sun" and appeared to thread their way along the Cascade peaks.

He told (the reporter) he timed how fast they flew between Mount Rainer and Mount Adams and came up with 1,200 mph. He added he could have been off by 200-300 mph, but "they were still the fastest things I ever saw."

The East Oregonian newspaper ran front page follow-ups June 27, 28 and 30 (June 29 was a Sunday, and the paper did not publish on Sundays), some stories with witnesses corroborating Arnold's account. "Flying disc" appeared in the June 27 Associated Press story, and the reporter used it in his story of June 28, but the phrase each time is in quotes without attribution.

The newspaper recorded that the term "flying saucers" finally showed up on June 30, 1947 in a short AP story about a La Grande reverend declaring the end of the world was "imminent" after residents there reported UFOs. The "strange zooming objects" – or flying saucers – according to Rev. Lester Carlson, were "the signs of the second coming of Christ."

From this point on, in 20th Century history, people began to believe in UFOs as signs of life from outside the universe.

Perhaps they weren't from outside the universe, but rather from another dimension within the universe. Perhaps what we experienced with Lafayette Backus involved the first mention of flying saucers or dimensional beings who came and went as they desired.

Ken Arnold's flight back to Boise, Idaho happened 113 years *before* Isaac Newton's date of 2060. And just four score and four years *after* meeting Abraham Lincoln.

Though separated by time and space, their fates would all be intertwined.

Section III

13

Choosing A. Lincoln

Doc's Vienna flat
1913

After Jack Lewis awoke and seemed accepting of knowing his own manner and day of death, our group left the Besso Brothers' flat, with Doc in the lead, Lewis near the end.

We walked the cobblestone streets of 1913 Vienna to Doc's townhouse. Different spacetime pivot-points were discussed, options were considered.

We discussed the malevolent intruder, about whom I wrote in my first volume, who kept making himself present to us at the café after the murders and beyond. He was with us and then he wasn't. In and out of time. A whisp of being, a gale force of negative spirit.

"That being presented a different sort of evil than I've ever encountered," said Putzi. "And I personally knew Adolf Hitler for many, many years. I saw his intense hatred, close up and privately. The type of focused malevolence in his eyes is the same type of hatred I saw in that being's eyes outside of Café Central."

"His presence provided a cascading sense of such destructive, demonic desire that I couldn't turn away, all the while finding myself sick to my stomach, as I stared at him," Louise said.

Zack injected, "What a creeper to the max – I mean, he appeared, did his destruction and then disappeared in front of you?"

Doc added, "Just as I lunged at him, trying to take a swing at his face."

I added, "He's got to be connected to Newton and the year 2060."

Doc said, "He is connected to Newton's prophecy about the end of the world. This being – and those that were alongside him, were not of this world, or better yet, they may have been of this world but not of this dimension."

Jack asked, "Could they be spirit beings?"

"Demonic spirit beings?" I asked.

"Yes, like those that I wrote about in the Silent Planet."

"Well, you tell me," Rick said more as a statement than a question.

"Do you mind me putting on my theologian hat, just for a short while?" Jack asked.

No one was opposed.

Jack began, "As a reader of the ancient manuscripts and a follower of Jesus, there can be no denying that the historical person who was born in Bethlehem, raised in Egypt and Northern Israel and who died in Jerusalem, was viewed traveling through walls, doors and time. Jesus spoke of light often, even saying he was The Light. Before his crucifixion, he met Moses and Elijah, all three clothed in brilliant white light as they stood on a hill top. Three witnesses saw them together. After he died, he was seen by over 500 witnesses and traveled in his own dimension of spacetime back and forth – eventually being with them for 40 days before he disappeared into the sky. Plenty of witnesses were at these events."

As we turned the corner onto Doc's street, Jack said, "There is definitely 'magic' afoot, about which we currently know very little. We'll move closer to it, just watch and see. And if there is the light of Jesus near us, there is the strong probability that other spirit beings – those from darkness – are also near us. From outer areas or from inner space."

We arrived at Doc's flat in short order and presented the broad options. My spacetime traveling team and I began researching additional items that might be important to a potential plan for delaying, if we can, any pending end-of-world disaster in 2060.

We discovered that the year 1860 (when Lincoln was elected) and 1960 (when Kennedy would be elected) were key to understanding 2060 (the year when Isaac Newton penned would be the earliest that the world could end). History as it is currently written *and* as a direct result of these two Presidents' deaths, would be creating intense leadership voids. Disallowing the future world of being able to solve vital problems, would hurtle the earth towards its mathematically calculated ending, as predicted by one of the most brilliant men who had ever lived, Sir Isaac Newton.

In 1704 Newton wrote, "It may end later, but I see no reason for its ending sooner than 2060." These two hundred years from 1860 to 2060 would be filled with utterly terrible events of death and destruction. Armed conflict, both civil war and international war would rip apart much of the world.

Yet there was hope, right in front of us – in the pages of history. The John Hay/John Nicolay ten volumes on Lincoln's life gave us an incredible body of options to consider about Lincoln, through almost 4,600 pages of content in ten volumes.

In the days to come we burrowed through those volumes, drew timeline maps on the sheets hung on the walls, looked at events in the 19th and 20th centuries, in anticipation of how to postpone Armageddon in the 21st century. We did so, day after day in Vienna in 1913.

For 12 long days. It helped that C. S. Lewis was with us. His research skills were incredible.

The result of our review began with Abraham Lincoln but also included other historical leaders; John F. Kennedy, the Rev. Martin Luther King, Jr. and U.S. Senator Robert F. Kennedy, brother of the president; as well, Civil War Generals ,John Sedgewick and George Custer would survive – one by intention, one by accident. Men whose shielding from gunshots would change the world.

The tactical nature of the plan involved President Kennedy escaping Dallas, Rev. King running for President and *not* stepping out on the balcony of the Lorraine Motel, Sen. Bobby Kennedy running for President *later* than 1968 and winning; Gen. Grant's absence from Custer's life and therefore by not returning to his troops on The Plains he would survive by default. We had already saved General John Sedgewick's life in our previous spacetime adventure. Now, they could all live and change history.

The starting point, though, was saving the life of President Abraham Lincoln.

Each day, we knew we became more successful working together as a group of researchers; the sheer volume of information was developed and key points were discovered or unveiled. Yet, we sensed we might need *at least* one additional researcher to join us with this project. The new member of our group needed to have intimate knowledge of Lincoln, and the international wars.

John Hay and John Nicolay's 10-volume work, *Abraham Lincoln A History,* held the key. Lincoln's two Private Secretaries were with him every day in the Civil War White House, making this collection of books a fascinating window through which we could, as eyewitnesses, review and study the 16th President.

Lincoln's rescue from death would have to be paramount in our research.

Rick said it best, when we took a break "Lincoln's death gave us Andrew Johnson, who had only been Vice President for 42 days. He was a foolish, uncouth man – in fact he was drunk when he was inaugurated!"

Louise asked Rick, "Wait, wasn't he Lincoln's Vice President the whole four years before?"

"Nope, that's what I'm telling you. Lincoln had an incredible man of integrity and knowledge during his first administration – Hannibal Hamlin from Maine and then he chose this contemptable man."

Louise continued, "You mean Lincoln dumped a perfectly fine incumbent Vice President in favor of a drunk?"

"Yeah, he did. It was a terrible decision, a moment of President Lincoln's worst display of weakness. He let the party bosses make the decision and they ingloriously ousted Hamlin."

Rick was showing his passion.

He continued, "Historians will explain away the decision as somehow important for national unity – a Southerner and a Northerner together, but they'd be wrong. Johnson brought the US to its knees after the Civil War and was the first president to be impeached in the House, though he missed conviction in the Senate by one solitary vote."

Jack entered into the discussion, "With us stopping Lincoln's assassination, not only will his life be saved but the United States Civil War would come to a far more peaceful end and by extension of that, a far better Reconstruction period in your nation's history would happen. The volatile racial tensions, that grew generation after generation, of the post-emancipation years could be more quickly met and resolved with a man like Lincoln, or even his first Vice President – Hannibal Hamlin – for that matter."

He paused, "We must keep reading through the research to see who might be our best choice to help save Lincoln's life." We all returned to our work.

It's important to note that the subsequent efforts in Europe to wage international war through genocide on the Jewish race would also be thwarted as the nations of the world chose not to embrace international violence. Ernst Rohm of Germany wasn't the only one who could avoid WWI, we determined; although *he* merely postponed the global conflict. The chain of leadership all returned to Lincoln. His continued life story would surely impact the 1870's, 80's and 90's for the better, we felt.

We would direct our efforts to end war altogether. Millions more would live; generation after generation would claim their own plots of ground on which they would safely and securely raise their families, rather than their burial plots. This could be done by eliminating the global conflict, that we historically have called WWI.

We would therefore ensure that WWII did not happen. As a group, we felt that that the termination of the Civil War and the elimination of any international wars would free people from slavery and death; we genuinely saw that this could be accomplished.

Rick Besso's military training and combat experience didn't dampen the spirit of peace that grew in our collective breasts. Instead, it strengthened us, "No one wants the elimination of armed conflict more than the soldier who fights in it," Rick simply stated.

Jack, himself a wounded British veteran from World War I, lit his pipe and at the same time gave a loud *huzzah*, "You are completely accurate, Lieutenant Colonel Besso."

The number of future individuals living in peace seemed to assure most of those in our group that we could avoid an apocalypse, or at the least *postpone* one for many decades, and maneuver for ourselves (and our posterity) more time on this earth. That was our hope – lessen war, increase peace. It became our guiding light.

We knew it wouldn't be easy, yet it could be simple. Most of life is just that. Death interrupts simplicity. And if we could help end that horrendously complex interruptive cycle of massive death, we could extend life.

First, we had to stop the single death of A. Lincoln.

U.S. Grant's book would be the key to accomplishing that, *or so we thought.*

14

Autographs and Counterfeits

1913 Vienna

It was Louise who first broached the possibility that our objective could *not* be reached.

"The plan is completely dependent on traveling through spacetime using the autographed two-volume set of Ulysses S. Grant's memoirs. *And those volumes will not help us.*"

We sat shocked.

Doc responded, "Louise, it makes *no* sense that we would *not* use the DNA from Grant's signature on his memoirs, to take us back in spacetime. He was with Lincoln repeatedly throughout the Civil War and was invited, but declined, to attend Ford's Theater on the evening of the president's assassination."

"And?" Louise asked.

I picked up the defense that Doc began, "And all we have to do is convince Grant to be with Lincoln that night, with additional guards and save his life."

Louise responded, "Yes, I understand all that. *I get it.* My point is that your whole argument rests on a faulty presupposition. Let me explain..."

"Please do," interrupted Putzi, as Jack, Zack and Rick looked on, intrigued.

"I didn't tell anybody, but during the last twelve days of research, I did something initially that was quite stupid...and then realized that it was a bit of a divine error of sorts."

"What do you mean? What did you do?' asked Doc.

Sheepishly, Louise glanced at the rug and then over to the table that held the two volumes of Grant's work. She rose from her chair moved to the table to pick up Volume 1. On the table also sat an empty glass. She pointed to the crystal tumbler, which still had a slight amount of clear liquid at the bottom.

"A week or so ago, I accidently bumped the table. This tumbler had more water in it. Volume 1 was laying open to Grant's signed page. The tumbler *sort of* earned its name when I bumped it and it tipped; water splashed onto Grant's signature..."

Rick and Zack both jumped to their feet.

"You did not!" Zack yelled. Rick steadied him with a quick brotherly hand on his shoulder.

Louise quickly responded, "*I did, I did,* but hold on – all of you. Listen to me. Nothing happened."

I entered the tense conversation, "What do you mean 'nothing happened'?"

"Nothing happened. Well, *almost* nothing. Certainly, the page was splashed by the water – and the signature received a potentially fatal dose of H2O, for such a small size of an autograph. As I immediately turned and grabbed for a small hand towel, I then turned back again to the page, expecting the ink to have 'run' and for it all to be a smeared-ink disaster."

She paused, "But it wasn't."

Doc responded, "What do you mean?"

"The ink did not run because it was not from a fountain pen, nor was it actually a real autograph. It was a facsimile signature printed by the publisher and dated May 23rd, 1885. Grant died on July 23rd, 1885."

Zack interrupted, "That date doesn't mean anything. There were still eight weeks between when the book was 'signed' and when he died. He could have signed it!"

Louise nodded her head and replied, "I read some further research by a future Lt. Governor of Idaho – attorney and historian David Leroy, who will become a prominent Lincoln scholar. He found that the book wasn't published until late 1885 and early 1886. The signature didn't run because Grant never touched this book, or any other book. He never signed them, because he had passed away so he could never have signed *our* volumes."

"Then how in the world did we use the book to travel to the Civil War and stop Union General John Sedgewick from being killed?" I asked.

Doc pointedly answered, "Because the signature of the first owner of the book, Orrin Backus, *was* real and we used *his* signature and DNA, not Grant's, to move us along Telluric Current One to the battlefield of Spotsylvania Court House. It was never Grant. It was always Backus."

Doc plopped himself into the large plush chair to the left. He was defeated.

Putzi, Zack and Rick sat taking it all in. They too seemed defeated.

Jack just listened; then he broke the silence. "So how do we return to Lincoln's time – to the White House of the early 1860's – and secure an audience with him? And who in the world do we use to gain entrance to Lincoln?"

Doc paused, thought about something and then jolted straight up, his air of defeat instantly cast aside. Louise also smiled widely.

Doc looked at her and joined her in her smile. They both had independently come to the same conclusion. He nodded in her direction, she turned toward us and answered, "Gentlemen, *and Zack...*" Everyone laughed, including Zack. "We're going to enter into A. Lincoln's world through a side entrance of his life – through the help of one of his personal secretaries – John Hay."

Doc ambled over to where the team had John Hay and John Nicolay's 10 volumes haphazardly spread over a huge table. He searched and found Volume 1, published in 1885, turned to the signature page that held Hay's autograph, dated 1904, with a short note addressed to the Republican Party. "To my friends who supported the Grand Old Party, on the 50th Anniversary of its founding – Under the Oaks, Jackson, Michigan, 1904."

Returning to Louise's tumbler, Doc dipped his right pinky finger in the slightly wet bottom of the crystal glass and dabbed the written period at the end of Hay's short written note: "Under the Oaks, Jackson, Michigan, 1904." The ink blurred immediately on the small period. The signature was authentic. The DNA was useable.

We were now headed back in time to 1904 to meet John Hay. From there, if our plan worked, we'd enlist Hay's help in saving the life of Abraham Lincoln before his assassination on April, 1865 occurred. Yet the nagging concern from 1947 remained about the malevolent dimensional characters, like Lafayette Backus, who entered into history though space and time, regardless of the year, regardless of a total lack of technology. Where had these forces of darkness come from?

Section IV

15

Pause to Consider

The 1800's and Unidentified Aerial Phenomena

For many centuries strange aerial visions in the sky happened across North and South America, Eurasia and Africa. Those who witnessed the speed of flights had no vocabulary with which to describe what they saw.

For context, the Wright Brothers would sail over Kitty Hawk five years into the 20th century – and then only at a speed of 6.8 miles per hour.

Years before the Wright Brothers, many wrote down in personal letters what they saw. Others gave reports to newspapermen at the time. Such as in Europe, "A dragon in the sky, traveling so fast that the speed would hurt one's ears."

There simply was no context in the lives of witnesses who lived prior to the 20th century for air travel or space travel. Yet there were odd beings on the earth, originating from the skies before mankind could fly in airplanes. The witnessing of these individuals and events were not solely limited to urban areas.

The indigenous people also saw themselves connected to the visitors from the sky and lived their lives accordingly, looking up.

They were looking for the Great Spirit in the Sky. At the beginning of the 19th Century, indigenous folklore and tribal experiences involved two types of visitors: small beings and incredible giants.

The 'Little People" stood about 18 inches tall and had remarkable gifts of healing, and as warriors of great strength against whom all other tribes were fearful to engage in combat. My own great-great-grandfather, and namesake, was William Clark. He and Meriwether Lewis met with tribal warriors who confirmed the existence of these small warriors. The leaders of the Sioux and Lakota tribes strongly directed Lewis and Clark NOT to go to the home of the fierce 'Little People'. However, ten men of Lewis and Clark's command joined them and investigated this strange and fearful mound area. The leaders of the tribes expected these white men to be killed. The dozen white adventurers saw Spirit Mound though they did not meet with the expected small warriors. They returned to their mission of reaching the Pacific Ocean, uninjured. The tales of the Little People did not disappear.

Notably, one of the famous Crow Indian leaders, Plenty Coups, as a nine-year-old boy met the Little People and had a vision in which the chief of the Little People took him into another dimension of time and space to a spirit-world lodge where he prophesied over the youth: that he would become the chief of the Crow nation.

Two years later, Plenty Coups had a second vision at age eleven involving the Little People. A voice told him that the buffalo would soon disappear and the white man's cattle would take their place. But that the Crow Nation would survive under his leadership and in time they would live as a nation near the exact spot mentioned in this vision. It all came true.

Giant beings were also spotted throughout the Plains, the Southwest and onto Catalina Island in what is now Southern California. The strength of these giant beings was marveled at (and feared) by indigenous tribes of all backgrounds. Proof of their existence was found throughout the entire United States.

For example, in 1959, the curator at the Carnegie Museum, unearthed a 7 feet 2-inch skeleton of an ancient indigenous male during the excavation of the Cresap Mound in Northern West Virginia. Sixty years earlier, in Miamisburg, Ohio the body of a man "more gigantic than any ever recorded in human history, was found in the Miami Valley. The skeleton, it is calculated, must have belonged to a man 8 feet 1.5 inches in height." Then again reports show, just off the coast of Southern California, "amateur archaeologist Ralph Glidden unearthed and collected a total of 3,781 skeletons on Catalina Island and the Channel Islands between 1919 and 1930 working for the Heye Foundation of New York. He unearthed several enormous skeletons measuring over 9 feet."

These giants matched the descriptions by Josephus in the Middle East – the Nephilim of antiquity. These beings apparently made both local and global migrations, surprising all who came in contact with them, due to their height and vicious behaviors. Josephus writes that from the creation of man, "For seven generations, these people continued believing in God as master of the universe, but fell into vice and depravity. Some born of angels who had consorted with women resembled the audacious giants of Greek mythology."

The ancient Hebrew Torah is even much more direct: "There were giants in the earth in those days; and after that, when the sons of God (fallen angels) came in unto (had sex with) the daughters of men, and they bare children to them… And God saw that the wickedness of man was great in the earth, and that every imagination of the thoughts of his heart was only evil continually."

In 1896 Colonel H.G. Shaw of Lodi, California was driving his buggy and came across an aircraft, the description of which matches many listed in modern day aerial phenomena sightings. His report stated that there were 7-foot-tall women standing on the spaceship. "They did not speak, but "warbled" to one another in a language he could not understand. Although they attempted to take Shaw, he was too heavy. The aliens floated away in their ship and he never saw them again." Throughout the latter 1890's "airships" were witnessed throughout the United States and other countries.

Airships had not yet been invented.

In 1969 at the direction of the Library of Congress for the Air Force Office of Scientific Research, Office of Aerospace Research directed researcher Lynn E. Catoe to compile a bibliography of sightings of spacecraft (and extra-terrestrial beings) in both antiquity and the mid-20th century. That bibliographical list of researched sightings is 400 pages long.

Among the scientific findings listed in her work for the Library of Congress was the treatise from early American historian Rushton M. Dormanfs on American Indian mythology and folklore, 'The Origin of Primitive Superstitions, published in 1881.' As well, from published works of Hansen L. Taylor: 'He Walked the Americas', published by Amherst Press in 1963. It was a collection of American Indian legends collected over many years – both old and new – that indigenous tribes and clans have passed down to subsequent generations.

Other evidence was cited as occurring in China by archeologists; hieroglyphics suggesting that extraterrestrial spacecraft landed on earth 12,000 years ago. Thousands of other additional global examples were listed in Ms. Catoe's bibliography.

How did these beings enter and exit with such ease into mankind's dimension? Physics demands obedience by all objects in this universe, but somehow these extra-terrestrials seemed to have been given a pass, travelling effortlessly into and out of our world. Respected journalist and long-time investigator John Keel disagreed that they are extra-terrestrials, having come from another planet to earth. Instead, he famously called them 'Trojan Horse ultra-terrestrials; believing they travelled effortlessly within and among the dimensions – and *not* from other planets.

In her Summary, Ms. Catoe from the Library of Congress stated, "Many of the UFO reports now being published in the popular press recount alleged incidents that are strikingly similar to demonic possession and psychic phenomena which have long been known to theologians and parapsychologists. Therefore, references to these subjects have been included as well as references to occult works which have similarities to the general tone and content of the UFO literature."

She ended her Summary with this statement: "Scientific theory of today often becomes fact tomorrow. The line between the possible and the impossible is arbitrary. Many misconceptions pass for information. One day, perhaps within our time, out of all the contradictions surrounding the UFO phenomenon, man may discover to his complete satisfaction its exact nature and origin.

-July 1969 LYNN E. CATOE"

Our investigation of dimensional spacetime travel demanded that we continue to move horizontally through time before we could investigate the vertical possibilities of ultra-terrestrials.

The most important man of the late 19th and early 20th centuries must first be met – John Hay, the man who walked with 'giants' of a different nature.

Section V

16

Meeting John Hay

1904

Doc, Rick, Zack, Louise, Putzi, Jack and I completed our travel from 1913 back to 1904; smoothly landing, we thought, in Jackson, Michigan, to meet John Hay.

We were wrong by a distance of 271 miles.

Though we knew it couldn't scientifically be so, Telluric Current 1 (TC1) appeared to take us off-course to the north to dock area of the The Grand Hotel on Mackinac Island in Northern Michigan's Upper Peninsula. The team climbed the long hill from where ships docked to the entrance of The Grand Hotel. I've been many places in my life and seen many beautiful architectural exterior facades. This hotel, built in the 19th century has by far one of the most impressive front porches and porticoes of any hotel I've ever seen: 660 feet long. It's the largest in the world. The hotel itself has almost ten acres under its many roofs. We climbed the front steps and entered the spacious main doors. The calendar in the main lobby of The Grand Hotel read July 3rd, 1904. Doc remained cool and collected as he surveyed the possibilities. We huddled in a couch area and Doc began to unpack why he believed we had overshot our destination by almost 300 miles and undershot it by 3 days and yet it was still *fine,* he said.

He began factually, "We are exactly where we should be. Facts don't lie." He paused, "John Hay's DNA from his autograph on Volume One of his book, Lincoln, A History, placed Hay here on this very date."

Putzi interrupted with touch of sarcasm, "How can you say that? We should be in Jackson, Michigan, not "Big Porch", Michigan…"

Jack Lewis stepped outside of the lobby area to wander on the porch, his pipe lit and his hands coupled together behind his back.

Doc acted as though he had not heard Putzi's question and comment.

"John Hay DID sign this copy of his book. And he DID it today – right here at this hotel. My reasoning is sound and is backed up by all we've gone through on so many occasions."

It was Louise's chance to interrupt, "In other words, had he not signed it here, we would have all gone to where he *did* sign it – which we thought would be Jackson, Michigan. But we didn't land there, so we are where we need to be…correct?'

Doc vigorously nodded yes while he moved towards the Main Desk. We followed him with our eyes and our ears.

Lewis returned to our group, seemingly astonished by both the telluric travel he had just experienced and by the beauty of The Grand Hotel. He approached Doc and quietly stood next to him.

"Excuse me, sir" Doc said to the concierge, "Would you mind ringing John Hay's room for me. My name is Dr. Russell Gersema and this is Jack Lewis.

"Ringing?" asked the man behind the long oaken bar-like Main Desk, with a look of confusion.

Doc paused and reconsidered the word he used for a telephone call. In 1904 phone lines came into a business or hotel, *but* extensions were less likely to be in use. A note would have to suffice.

"Oh, pardon me, I should have known. Would you mind sending a bell hop to Colonel Hay's room with a note that Dr. Gersema, of Vienna, Austria is in the lobby and would like to have a moment with him?'

The concierge wrote the note and dispatched the bellhop.

Doc redirected us back to the overstuffed Victorian couches and chairs off to the side, by the large front, plate glass window.

Zack put into words what we all were wondering, "Do we still have to be in Jackson on July 6th?

"I don't think so," Doc responded.

"Why did we choose 1904 to intersect John Hay? And why in Jackson, Michigan *or here,* for that matter?" Zack asked quickly, anticipating Colonel Hay's arrival, from down the incredibly long main hallway of The Grand Hotel.

Rick instinctively reacted, "I'm not sure what you're going to say, Doc, but as a part of this trip, we're finally going to end the debate that Zack and I've had for years."

We all turned toward him for an explanation. Louise looked particularly inquisitive.

Zack smiled and said, "Is that so?"

Rick responded, "Yep, remember, 'Ripon or Jackson'?"

Zack chuckled and said, "I remember the $10,000 you'll owe me if it was Ripon, Wisconsin or that God-forsaken little village of Jackson, Michigan."

Louise couldn't remain silent anymore. "What are you two buffers talking about?'

Both men looked at her and then at each other. "Buffers?"

Louise said the word again as though everyone should know what it meant, *"Buffers."*

Zack responded, "Yeah, we heard the word, but what the heck *is* a buffer?'

Louise answered, "Come on, *don't sell me a dog…* you two. I'm *getting the Morbs from you."*

This was the first time that any of us had seen either Zack *or* Rick speechless.

Louise, added, "I half expect one of you to start another food fight." Then she smirked and continued, "What is it you are comparing between Wisconsin and Michigan?"

Rick shook off his mental floss confusion about her expressions and responded, "Ok, ok, here's the deal. My brother and I have had a $10,000 bet for years on *where* the Republican Party of the United States, *the GOP,* started. It should be simple but it's not. He says Rippon, Wisconsin and I say Jackson, Michigan." Then he looked over at his brother who sat shaking his head, mumbling negative comments about his brother grousing over the long-held bet.

Rick responded, "Well, *little brother*, today we'll settle that bet."

Before either Doc or I could add our comments to the debate, Putzi interjected, "Ja, and why this particular man? Sure, he was Lincoln's stenographer…"

Rick interrupted, "What? He was President Lincoln's *private secretary.* You know, like his administrative assistant – a sort of chief of staff – although they didn't have that position in the 1860's presidency. There were two other private secretaries, as well – Hay's friend John G. Nicolay and a guy named Stoddard. In fact, Nicolay was the one who obtained the presidential campaign job *for* Hays, which later led to the White House years and the Civil War. Nicolay was Hay's boss, though both were close friends."

And Doc chimed in, "I brought three books with me in my satchel: obviously we traveled here on Telluric Current One because of the autograph in John Hay's book; but I also brought my copy of Philip McFarland's remarkable book, John Hay – Friend of Giants, as it's one of the best biographies on Hay, along with John Taliaferro's book, *All the Great Prizes.* I did so if we need to use them to convince Mr. Hay that we are truly from the future."

Zack said, as a snarky aside, "Thanks Doc for book club referrals, but we've got our work cut out for us when we meet Mr. Hay and then get him to..."

Rick cut his brother off mid-sentence, "Colonel Hay."

"What?"

"He preferred 'Colonel Hay'.

"Wait, what class at West Point *was* Hay?" Zack asked.

Rick responded, "He wasn't. He received his commission, in his twenties, directly from President Lincoln during the Civil War. Then he served some key missions on behalf of the President and kept his rank for the rest of his life."

Rick added, "Um, Colonel John Hay is the invited guest of honor of the Republican National Committee to speak on July 6th at the…*get this, Zack…* 50th Anniversary event for the founding of the Grand Old Party in 1854 in Jackson, Michigan…"

Zack looked soberly at his brother, paused an inordinate amount of time and said very slowly, "Wager won. 10,000 George Washingtons are coming your way."

Rick smiled. It was a somewhat painless end to a long-standing painful debate between the brothers. And that was that.

Doc pulled out his glasses along with the two biographical books on Hay and read first from McFarland's book, "Now, perhaps only those enmeshed in nineteenth-century American history know his name; but when John Hay died in 1905…"

Putzi interrupted, "That's a year from now!"

Doc gave him a look, over his reading glasses, as if to say, 'No further interruptions.' It worked.

He continued reading out loud, "'…but when John Hay died in 1905, in his sixty-seventh year… he was one of the most famous men in the world.'"

Keeping an index finger in the spot he was reading yet closing the book slightly, Doc turned to us, "By the end of his life – the very period of time in which we find ourselves *today* – Hay was personal friends with President Theodore Roosevelt, Mark Twain, Horace Greeley and many others. He had been Secretary of State for two Presidents and therefore, with the vacancy of the office of Vice President occurring twice under those two men, Hay was twice put in the direct line of succession to become President of the United States."

Louise shook her head in disbelief, "Who IS this guy?"

17

The Man Who Could Have Been President...Twice

1904 Jackson, Michigan

"I'm not done yet," Doc spit out, "He was a favorite of Queen Victoria, spent time as a diplomat in Paris, Vienna and Madrid, perfected French and German and had a working knowledge of Spanish."

Doc reopened McFarland's book and read "The sun shone down on this capable gentleman...finding ample time for leisure, and marveling at his lifelong good fortune. Yet one more example of his good fortune: at the start of the 1860's – or just before – young Hay, fresh out of college, dejected, unsettled in life, had a rare good fortune (no doubt the greatest luck that ever befell him) at age twenty of finding himself, for lack of anything better to do, reading law in a lawyer uncle's office in Illinois. Lucky for Hay that the year was the one it was; and lucky that his Uncle Milton's practice was on the same floor and next door to that of a couple of other lawyers – Lincoln & Herndon, Attorneys. And extremely lucky for John Hay that the senior member of the neighboring law firm was just then coming into his own on the national political stage."

All of us just took a breath.

Jack Lewis spoke first. "Was it really luck? I mean, it sounds like John Hay had a destiny set before him by God, and he followed it."

I added my thoughts, "I agree. I mean, *come on,* at twenty years of age he's asked by his older, close friend, Nicolay, to come to work for Candidate Abraham Lincoln; and then, when Lincoln wins the Presidency, he moves with Nicolay, and that other guy Stoddard, into The White House!"

Putzi added, "Everything I've read in Hay and Nicolay's autobiographical works says that they felt that *your* President Lincoln treated these young men as if they were his *own* sons. Am I mistaken?"

Rick Besso answered, "You are correct. In fact, as Zack and I were growing up, we both had an interest in in Civil War history; we studied and researched the sons whom Lincoln actually did have."

Putzi said, "What did you find?"

Zack responded, "Lincoln's firstborn son, Robert was the only son who grew to adulthood. He watched as each of his younger brothers passed away – Eddie, just before his own fourth birthday; Willie just after he turned eleven; and Tad died a couple months after he turned eighteen in 1871, just six years after his father's assassination. By the loss of his father and his final brother, Robert Lincoln, at twenty-eight, was virtually an orphan."

Louise responded, "What terrible sadness for a family to endure; what deep sadness for the older brother to live with the rest of his life! Were Robert, John Hay and John Nicolay friends?"

Doc answered, "Yes, close friends. In fact, on the night of the assassination Robert and John were playing cards and drinking together at the White House when they received word of the President's shooting. They rushed to his bedside for what became the death vigil."

I looked at the ceiling, recalling the loss of my own wife from cancer and could only say, "Death of loved ones is an amputation, a brutal painful amputation. It's just so permanent," I paused, "until it isn't, in some cases..."

"What do you mean?", Doc asked softly.

"Well, we've learned that spacetime travel can be manipulated so that when a person accidentally dies, he or she could be allowed to live, should circumstances be changed. I mean it's why we went to Vienna and tackled the tyrants. That's why we're here in Michigan in 1904. Diseases, cancer, etc. are often held within the person, sometimes carried for years until the inevitable happens."

He nodded.

Jack nodded as well.

Rick picked up the conversation and continued, "So it is, with our task before us. Hay was at Lincoln's bedside when he died. We'll help Hay and then have him help us. It's got to be our *combined* plan to save the President from the derringer ball that was fired into his skull by John Wilkes Booth. We intend to keep him alive until the natural termination of his life, right?"

I nodded.

Zack added, "And by doing that, we'll ensure that Hay joins us for the bigger picture of slowing the pace of how quickly the world will accelerate towards the near-Armageddon of the twentieth century's two world wars... and then Armageddon, itself, after 2060."

Short-lived silence enveloped us.

Louise broke that silence, "So, getting back to the main purpose for why we are *under the oaks* in Michigan in 1904..."

From his satchel Doc simply took out again *Volume One of Lincoln – A History*, flipped to the autograph with date and place penned under it in Hay's own handwriting. Dr. Russell Gersema said, "Let's invite John Hay to join us and change the world by saving Abraham Lincoln's life."

A dapper man in his late-60's with a very well barbered beard approached our group, with a book tucked under his left arm. "Good afternoon, I'm Colonel John Hay and I'm looking for Dr. Russell Gersema of Vienna, Austria," he said as he extended his right hand toward us.

18

John Hay Joins Us

1904 Michigan and 1863 Washington, D.C.

It's a strange and magical thing to watch something like scales fall from a person's eyes.

After moving from the main lobby to John Hay's suite at the Grand Hotel on Mackinac Island in upper Michigan that very magic began to happen. I had earlier experienced this feeling with Putzi and Louise when I saw Doc explain to them the principles of spacetime travel. I also experienced this with Orin Backus and Mark Twain, during our first journey, about which I previously wrote.

In a real sense it's like being an observer in a patient's room as a PA or a chiropractor adjusts or manipulates the spine. As expert Dr. Kevin Hearon, D.C. explains the phenomena, "At just the moment when a vertebra is moved back into place, the pockets of air are released and there's often an audible sound – a sort of *pop* – and there's an observable look of relief in the eyes of the patient. An *uncomfortable comfort,* of sorts."

In a real sense I experienced this earlier as Dr. Russell Gersema unpacked spacetime travel for me. More so, when I actually traveled through space and time.

With John Hay, it was a different kind of the same.

Doc unpacked the whole principle of spacetime travel and how the mechanics of travel work. Once trust was gained, John Hay was absorbed by the scientific lesson. We sat for almost an hour in the lobby lounging area of The Grand Hotel while John Hay, the most famous man in the world, during the 19th century, heard and felt the *pops* occur in his mind and spirit as he learned about spacetime travel.

The key to Hay believing this tale were the copies Doc brought of McFarland's book, *John Hay Friend of Giants,* published in 2017 and Taliaferro's 2013 book, *All the Great Prizes*. Doc showed him the covers, the publishing pages with the Library of Congress numbers on them and the table of contents for both books. Doc purposely did not place the books in Hay's hands – so that the final chapters, with descriptions of his death, could be read. Hay did notice something else – a quote on the page opposite the table of contents on McFarland's book. He read it out loud.

"'I have been extraordinarily happy all my life. Good luck has pursued me like a shadow…' John Hay to Henry Adams, July 11th, 1901", he paused, then looked up from the page, "I wrote that to my friend and neighbor just after the death of my only son, Adelbert." A lengthy pause ensued, "We called him Del." Hay choked up, "My son had just accepted the position of assistant secretary to President McKinley – the same post I held under President Lincoln – when, one night in New Haven, Connecticut, he accidently fell 60 feet from a third-floor window of his hotel and… perished." Hay's tears flowed in complete sadness. His heaving and sobbing filled our space.

Jack remained quiet as he observed the deep emotion.

Louise moved closer to Hay and put her arm around him. He did not pull back. We joined them by embracing the sadness. We asked Colonel Hay to tell us about his son. In doing so, we heard his love and his passion for Del flow.

"I, uh, I wrote that sentence to Henry Adams to express the fact that 'luck' was my constant companion, *until it wasn't.* The next sentence in the actual letter said 'Now it is gone – it seems to me forever. I expect tomorrow to hear bad news, something insufferable.'"

Doc quietly moved us to the large dining room to change the course of discussion and to further fill in the blanks for John Hay to better understand the opportunities that were in front of us for spacetime travel.

That afternoon, it took *one name* and *one personal experience* from Doc, along with *two questions* from Hay, for the current Secretary of State under President Theodore Roosevelt to ultimately see the veracity of spacetime travel, and the subsequent opportunity set before us.

The *one name* was Mark Twain.

John Hay and our dear friend and fellow spacetime traveler, Sam Clemens, were born three years and 45 miles apart from one another near the banks of the Mississippi River; Clemens in Hannibal, Missouri and Hay in Warsaw, Illinois. However, they first actually met in their twenties, in the late winter of 1867 in New York City. Their careers and interests eventually wound around one another for decades, just as the shoreline of the Mississippi River that connected their early lives wound around them. Hay knew Clemens very well.

The *one personal experience* was next.

So much so, that Doc turned to Putzi Hanfstaengl and had him relay how Putzi first met Mark Twain in Vienna's Café Central. Everything Putzi said in German made John Hay sit up, take notice and, in a most astonishing way, acknowledge that the story had to be true. Putzi placed an old frayed book on the table next to him and leaned forward.

Putzi finished in English, "So you see, Herr Secretary of State, I accidentally spewed coffee all over Sam's beautiful white suit, when I realized that your friend and mine, Mark Twain, was challenging me three years after history recorded his death! And yet there he was, requoting himself to us that his death was "still greatly exaggerated"!

Hay howled and quickly responded, "That response is pure 'Sam Clemens', through and through!"

And then, suddenly, "He was alive after he died?"

Hay became stone cold motionless in response.

Putzi leaned back and lit one of his European cigarettes and blew smoke toward the high ceiling. "More than that…Sam went from being a most terribly negative man at the end of his life to a man with hope and a direction forward because of traveling through spacetime. We sent him back to his past with specific directions to follow, to avoid financial collapse and to enjoy life and write from his soul. He became more than alive."

Hay responded, "My heavens, Sam indeed became one of the richest men in America. He and his wife, Livy, reside in Hawaii and own vast tracks of land and most of the shorelines on the majority of the islands."

Putzi blew another plume of blue smoke into the air, with a semi-arrogant yet all-knowing single word of response: "Excellent!"

Hay followed up, as if speaking only to himself, "You both went through time with Sam. You went forward in time and you went backward in time. You changed Sam's life?"

We nodded in agreement.

Then he suddenly paused.

"Dr. Gersema…"

"Please call me Doc. That'll be fine."

"Alright, Doc, I have *two questions.*"

"Go ahead."

"*My first question* is this: why did you come to Mackinac Island to The Grand Hotel, to see me?"

Doc responded, “That’s an easy one to answer. We didn’t mean to…”

Hay reacted, “What?”

Doc responded, “That’s not completely accurate. We *did* come to see you; we just hadn’t planned on arriving at The Grand Hotel to do so. We used the one autographed copy of your first volume of ‘Lincoln, A History’ to get to wherever you were when you signed it.” He handed the aged copy to Hay, and continued, “Which we thought was Jackson, Michigan.”

Hay received the old, frayed book copy and examined it with great interest, turning it open to the flyleaf page and seeing his own fading signature and the words,’ Jackson, Michigan – the GOP’s first 50 years, July 6th, 1904.’ With a barely discernable fingerprint smudge of ink under the signed name.

“Wait,” he turned briskly and retrieved the book he’d set on the table between himself and Putzi. It was fresh and new. It was the very same copy of the aged book that Doc had allowed him to examine. “This is the very same book…” He offered it to me.

I took the book and opened it to the flypage. There was the exact same wording. I touched it and withdrew my finger quickly, as if burnt. The ink was still slightly damp.

The fingerprint ink smudge near the signature was mine! Hay looked stupefied. We all did. Zack broke the silence, “And your *second* question?”

19

Can You Save My Son?

1904 Michigan

Snapping back, as though from an incredible distraction, Hay responded, "If you saved Mark Twain's finances, and you plan on saving Abraham Lincoln's life, my question is this: can you save the life of my son, Del? He fell to his death from an open window in 1901 at Yale University, not too long after his graduation from there."

Doc paused, looked around at all of us, especially at Jack Lewis, and then looked into John Hay's eyes.

"Yes, I believe we can do that, but in saving both men's lives it may just involve you losing all that you've gained and also ending Mr. Lincoln's political career and place in history."

The horvat-wrinkles on the sides of John Hay's eyes crinkled slowly as he squinted. He waited and then thoughtfully responded, "they say that politics, like life, may indeed allow second acts. Abraham Lincoln's life, as President, had no such luck… nor did the life of my son…till now… and if the cost to me of a second act ends up being poverty and ignominy, I don't care."

He paused again. Jack Lewis spoke. "Colonel Hay, I have long been a believer of Mr. Lincoln because of the work that you and Mr. Nicolay did with your 10-volume biography on him. I am more deeply a believer in the God who made us all. He holds our lives in his hands and in the case of those who follow him, he also allows magic to occur – the simple act of miracles."

Jack adjusted his glasses and continued, "I'm a novice to spacetime travel, but this I know, somehow in God's creation and in his history, he has allowed time and space to occasionally part, to morph. This appears to be one of those miraculous times."

Then, with a deliberate sort of forward motion in his body and in his speech, Hay said, "Yes, I want to help both of them live… to see Mr. Lincoln's family – his son, Robert, mature and to see Mr. Lincoln himself grow older with his wife, Mary. To see my own son, Del, become the *true* winner of all the great prizes; I will ransom my life's success for that. Without hesitation, *yes*."

20

The Grand Hotel, Mackinac Island

1904

The Grand Hotel on Mackinac Island in 1904 was gorgeous. We spent time on the east end of huge main porch, working on our plans.

John Hay's most important request would be granted and our first part of the plan was set.

Saving Del's life would prove to be the simpler of the two plans. Doc assigned Rick and Zack to that duty and they immediately began the needed actions to utilize DNA from Del's signature on a single page letter his father kept folded in his wallet – the last letter from Del to his father, written the day of his death.

After tucking McFarland's book under his arm and departing the hotel, the Brothers Besso headed back to the spot near the shoreline where we originally arrived. Hay, Louise and I accompanied them to the shoreline. Rick, along with Zack vanished, by Telluric Current One, headed to New Haven, Connecticut in late June, 1901, almost three years in the past.

John Hay stood in amazement as they disappeared, and in utter anticipation he said out loud, as much to himself as to anyone of us, “Godspeed, gentlemen, please save my son’s life.”

We returned to the Grand Hotel and sat with the others in a kind of holy silence until Hay shook himself awake and brought us back to our second part of the mission before us.

“All right… let’s save the life of President Lincoln,” he said.

Doc and I responded and presented what we thought would next need to occur.

Hay listened intently to Doc and me as we detailed the second plan – to go back to April of 1865 and stop John Wilkes Booth and his conspirators from carrying out the assassination of the President. Doc and I shared a deep level of awareness from historical research of the specific events that happened on the evening Abraham Lincoln was murdered. Over one hundred and fifty years had elapsed (for those of us from the 21st Century), however for Hay, Louise and Putzi it had been only thirty-nine years. The Secretary of State and part of our group were closer to the event in emotional experience, than were we. Lincoln was his friend and benefactor, their hero.

We produced the plan, full of actions/responses and needfully well-timed counter responses to the assassins’ plans. We would do *this* with each of the conspirators and we would do th*at* with the Pinkerton guards assigned to guard the president. Each part of the plan seemed like a choreography of defensive parries, slightly shaded by an occasional offensive thrust. All very complicated, all very dependent on what we felt we knew from having read about the assassination from Hay’s own works on Lincoln’s last hours.

Having explained the full plan in detail, Doc and I sat back and awaited Hay’s response. Hay suggested that we all walk around the lovely grounds of the Grand Hotel, getting some exercise and talking without the chance of being overheard in the dining room or becoming lethargic in Hay’s suite. We needed to clear our minds.

The grounds of the Grand Hotel are exceptional; huge areas of flowering plants, incredible shade trees and a rich, thick lawn of deep green fescue that spreads out everywhere.

Hay was measured in his responses, as we walked, "Yes, we can stop the assassins in their tracks and fully protect and save The Tycoon." At first, it seemed he was talking to himself; distant and not fully seeing the possibility of success as per the particulars of this plan.

Louise reacted to his strange comment and interrupted our thoughts, "Who?"

Hay blushed and responded, "Oh, my error. *The President.*"

Jack Lewis pushed further, "But you said The Tycoon. Why?"

Louise leaned forward.

Hay explained, "Yes, well, when Nicolay and I were his private secretaries, he referred to us as his *Boys* and *well* we referred to him by a name that had just entered the American language a few years earlier, I believe in 1857 when Commodore Perry returned from Japan, having negotiated with the supreme Japanese leader, the *taikun*. In America, that word became *tycoon* – which the two of us, as his secretaries regularly applied in private to President Lincoln, much to his delight."

Hay's unintentional, yet brief, smile radiated warmth by the memory and the sweet joy it brought back to him.

Louise seemed to take advantage of this interrupted personal moment; she seemed to have something different in mind. Turning to Doc, Hay and me she held up her right hand, as a crosswalk guard might do, allowing a different flow of people to move in a different type of direction, corner to corner.

She began, "I understand your reasoning for selecting, and possibly agreeing on, the actual day of President Lincoln's assassination for us to act and save his life, but I believe it's too dangerous, too much of a gamble. One slip-up and Lincoln's fate is again sealed by murder. There are simply too many moving parts in a flow of history that is so chaotic and crammed into such a small a period of hours, if not minutes."

Hay looked at Louise in a quiet and questioning way, as we walked along the shoreline near where we'd seen the Brothers Besso disappear just a short while ago.

He spoke up, "What do you suggest then?"

Louise looked at Doc and me, as if to seek our approval to spring something new on all of us, but not yet. Putzi looked on with interest, anticipating Louise's response.

Louise took a deep breath, closed her eyes and then began to say something.

Suddenly, she was interrupted by the combined swoosh of time travel, light and sound – the Brothers Besso arrived in our midst with the intense sense of a rushing wind behind themselves.

21

Returning from the Future

1903

Rick and Zack had been gone for less than an hour of actual time in Michigan in 1903. Yet, we'd come to find out that they'd been gone for many months in 1901 time.

John Hay moved quickly to them upon their arrival, saying in an almost uncontrollable way, "My son, my son... did you save his life?"

Zack smiled and shook off the slight time travel landing fatigue as he stood on the shoreline of Lake Huron and looked to his brother. Rick took the lead. "Colonel Hay, Del is alive. We stopped his accidental death from happening and he is alive and well in Washington D.C. occupying the very same position that you held under President Lincoln – assistant secretary to the President."

John Hay collapsed into a heap on the shoreline of deep green grass and light brown sand, with the smile of a Biblical father who received back his son from the dead. He clapped his hands together over his head and then held them in prayer-like fashion next to his chest and said amid tears, "My Del is alive!!"

Then he paused, gathering himself and looked at the Besso Brothers, "Tell me how you did it, please?" We all joined John Hay in sitting in the shoreline grass and beach sand, listening.

Rick again took the lead, "We arrived in New Haven, Connecticut the day before the "death date" of Del. It was morning and he had just written that letter to you, Colonel Hay. In fact, he had his version of the letter in his hands as he came to answer our knock at the door to his hotel room."

Zack added, "Your son's an amazingly warm and kind man, Colonel. Quite a big dude, man."

Hay smiled the smile all proud parents have when a compliment is given to their progeny.

Rick continued, "He opened the door and greeted us warmly as we explained that we had been sent by his father," both brothers nodded to John Hay, who nodded back to them, "and we asked if we could have 20 minutes of his time to show him something. He explained that he was just headed to the hotel front desk to find an envelope and send off the letter he held in his hand in the morning post."

Zack added, "Tucked in our possession, we held your original copy of the folded-up version of that very same letter – the one that you've carried in your wallet; the one we all used to transport us back to Del. However, we didn't show it to him at first, as we initially conversed. It seemed so strange that he held the same letter in his own hands, still slightly wet with ink, unfolded."

The Colonel looked like a young child on Christmas, walting for a gift to be unwrapped.

"I know, I know! We were about to blow his mind…" Zack stated plainly.

Louise saw John Hay's confusion at the term Zack just used and quickly interrupted, as if translating for the benefit of clear understanding, "Zack means that he and Rick were about to change Del's worldview and understanding of time and space – just as we have done for you. I *also* learned that strange expression from Doc. He blew my own mind." She smiled at Doc and he returned her smile in kind way.

Hay nodded fully aware of what both Louise and Zack were saying. "OK, I get it now. Thanks, please continue."

Rick picked up on the cue and continued, "We sat down next to the infamous open window, through which he could soon fall to his death. I glanced out of it towards the pavement and gave an unexpected shiver. Del, seeing the shiver, asked if I wanted the window closed. I said 'yes', if only for Del's benefit, for several hours from now."

Zack began, "Rick did a masterful job of finding common ground with Del, explaining that he was a graduate of West Point – which made Del smile, since that previous November Yale football lost to Army, 0-18 at West Point. Del asked if he could take a look at Rick's West Point Class Ring; he noticed the year on the ring. 1978 – seventy-seven years into the future. Then he paused and looked up at us. It was at that point that Rick handed McFarland's book – the one, Colonel Hay, that you reviewed – and he said one simple sentence to Del." Zack handed off the story to his brother.

Rick picked it up, "I told him what history told us – he would later that night be so tired that while sitting on the window sill, he would fall asleep and then fall to his death. That his soul would be required of him before God Almighty."

Hay said, "How did Del respond?"

"Just as any one of us would. He was seriously perplexed and immediately confused and looked at us as if we could be crazy. He's quite an analytical fellow. I thought the book and the class ring would do the trick, but they only pushed him deeper towards confusion. So, I withdrew from my coat pocket his slightly aged one-page letter to you (the one you've had in your wallet for three years) and placed it on the writing table between us., next to the now-closed window. Then I asked him to show me what he had just written to you that morning. He laid his fresh, unwrinkled letter next to the one I laid down. Word for word, the same. Penmanship, the same. They were identical letters except for one slight difference – one was old and one was new."

We were all quiet.

Zack spoke up. "We *really* blew his mind, *dude.*"

John Hay erupted in laughter. We all did.

Zack continued "And our twenty-minute meeting lasted for much longer as we unpacked the specifics using, of course, Philip McFarland's incredible book."

Rick gently turned to John Hay, 'friend of giants' from the 19th and early 20th centuries and said in a loving tone, "We saved your son, Colonel Hay. Will you now help us save your President?"

In tears, seated with his forearms on his bent knees, as he leaned forward in the sand of Lake Huron's shore, John Hay peered up and into each of our faces, scanning this small band of spacetime travelers, and said, "Abraham Lincoln shall indeed live."

Louise reached out and touched Hay's forearm, "I was interrupted when Zack and Rick returned with news of Del's life. May I now tell you how I think we should save Mr. Lincoln's life?"

Hay nodded. Doc and I did too. Putzie, Zack and Rick refocused on Louise.

She rose, dusted off sand from her palms as she placed them on her hips; looking at us as though we were students and she a teacher, Louise then lifted her right hand with the thumb and two fingers, in a European fashion, and said, "Three words."

She looked around at us.

"Impeachment and Conviction."

22

Convicting Lincoln

1903 The Grand Hotel, Michigan

"The argument is actually quite simple," Louise stated as she began elaborating on those previous three words, 'impeachment and conviction'.

"It won't be easy, but it could be simple."

We walked around the grounds of the Grand Hotel on Mackinac Island in the Upper Peninsula of Michigan in 1904, heading to the main entrance of the hotel and then into the magnificent lobby. Our discussions were intense and respectful. Impeachment and conviction of President Abraham Lincoln? It seemed unconscionable to me.

John Hay invited us all back to his suite and ordered room service. Our tasks were about to be reviewed and finalized, given the suggested plan by Louise.

The discussion surrounding Louise's proposal lasted several hours, reviewing the reasons that would allow the initiation of an impeachment and conviction during Lincoln's presidency.

This involved presenting the idea of returning *not* to the year 1865 before Lincoln's assassination but instead returning to the year 1863 of Lincoln's lowest point in the Civil War, Louise had mapped out a methodology of how Lincoln's life could be saved through impeachment and conviction; and the United States could avoid the final two years of intense bloodshed and death.

Rick Besso seemed to come alive at this combined prospect and quickly gravitated toward the premise and plan of Louise. John Hay cautiously joined them by listening and considering this option. Jack Lewis expressed the core thought that motivated us all, "The man-Lincoln must live, even at the expense of the myth-Lincoln. I support Louise's plan."

I remained unconvinced.

Rick said, "So, Louise, the plan as you've helped us better understand it is that you believe *Abraham* Lincoln's life would be *saved* by *ending President* Lincoln's political career?

Louise responded, "Not just that, but the aftermath of chaos that was caused by 'drunk Andy Johnson', Lincoln's Vice President would cease. There would be no Reconstruction nightmare."

Doc interrupted, "That doesn't make any sense! The President leaves earlier in disgrace and America *still* gets 'drunk Andy Johnson' – only now, earlier than expected after Lincoln is impeached in the House and convicted in the Senate?"

Rick launched in, "Not at all, Doc! Andrew Johnson was selected as Lincoln's *second* Vice President – and he'd only been in office some 40 days when the assassin's derringer ball extinguished the life of Mr. Lincoln and elevated Johnson to President."

Putzi jumped in, "So who was the *first* Vice President of *your* Mr. Lincoln?"

Hay looked down at the ground, a flicker of shame and embarrassment crossed his face, "His name was Hannibal Hamlin… and he served The Tycoon with honor, respect and loyalty." He remained looking down.

Putzi continued, "Well, if he was so respected and loyal, why was he *dishonored* and ejected from Abraham Lincoln's ticket for reelection in 1864?"

Hay looked up and said, as if hoping no one could really hear him, "People did that. People got him replaced."

Zack jumped in, "Who? What people?"

Hay's volume increased, "People in the Lincoln administration helped get him taken off the ticket in 1864."

Zack crumpled his face, as he moved inches from Hay's countenance and said, "People like you? Did you get rid of Hannibal Hamlin?"

Hay said nothing, but kept looking down at the floor.

Zack amped up, "*What a douche.* Really, you 'cut the throat' of a loyal VP… to gain what?" he continued without expecting an answer from Hay. "To get a guy who was drunk during his Inauguration Day address and then drunk on power from that point on? I mean people hated Johnson and he was the first President impeached, *man.*"

Zack looked at Rick and then delivered the kill shot, "Dude, if your son knew what you did to Lincoln's first V.P., he'd be ashamed of you!"

Hay's slumped body language said it all.

From where she was seated next to Hay's collection of his volumes of the Lincoln book Louise reached over and retrieved a volume. She began flipping the pages in search of something.

Hay still said nothing, then looked into Zack's face as if to distract the group, "How dare you use my son in this discussion."

People seated in nearby chairs responded to the increase in volume during this argument.

Zack lowered his voice and responded, "Look man, we went back through time to save your son's life. We. Did. It."

Zack's intensity was focused. "We have a vested interest in ensuring that your son holds you in an appropriate and honest perspective. And if you 'know in your knower' that you screwed this other dude, Hamlin, then just confess it now and we'll make amends. We have the opportunity to do that."

Hay was furious. He attempted to shift the argument. "You called me a *douche.*" Then he paused to collect himself. "What sense does that mean in this conversation? We're not discussing cleaning bodily orifices with streams of water."

Louise stopped and looked up disgusted from scrutinizing her copy of Volume 9 of the Lincoln biography. She asked, "Yes, what *are* you trying to say, Zack? I didn't quite understand your term, either."

Zack blushed, not quite wanting to deal with embarrassing a Victorian-era female.

She continued, "Well, Zack, what did you mean by that?'

Rick jumped into the verbal confusion. This was another one of those communication gaps that continually happen in spacetime travel. The confusing fluidity of language happens without people ever realizing it.

"That word won't take on any cultural significance until a book is published just after WWII called *From Here to Eternity.*" Rick paused and looked at Hay and Louise. "Indeed, it's a negative term. So, allow me to put it in late 19th Century parlance." Rick focused on Hay and said, "Colonel Hay… you were 'like Thomson's colt'."

Hay took immediate offense, and turned toward Rick and then toward Zack, "How dare the both of you!"

The people of 1904 seated in those nearby chairs and sofas awkwardly adjusted themselves, so that their bodies faced away from the confrontation but their ears maintained a clear access to the increasing volume.

We all looked surprised at Hay's harsh defensive reaction to such a strange and seemingly obtuse expression, at least it was *to us.* But not to Rick, who continued, "Yes, indeed, Colonel Hay, you were like Thompson's colt… such an infernal idiot, that you swam across the river to get a drink of water."

23

Hannibal Hamlin, Lincoln's Vice President

1904 The Grand Hotel, Michigan

Louise interrupted the translated linguistic fencing match. "Wait a minute, in your work on Lincoln's life, you said this – finding the page she had been searching for, "'There was nothing more before the Convention but the nominations, and one of those was already made.'" She interjected, "Lincoln."

Then she continued reading, "'The only delay in registering the will of the Convention occurred as a consequence of the attempt of members to do it by *irregular* and *summary* methods. Mr. Delano of Ohio made the customary motion to proceed to the nomination; Simon Cameron moved as a *substitute* the renomination of Lincoln and Hamlin by acclamation.'" She brought the still-open book down to her lap.

"That means that the whole convention would simply vote *aye*… and Lincoln and Hamlin would together again be the nominees, correct?" she asked as she stood to her feet.

Hay nodded and then motioned for the volume Louise now held on her lap. She handed it to him and he turned effortlessly to pages *past* where she had just read; he poked the page and then the paragraph with his right index finger and motioned Louise to continue reading.

She looked down, found the spot and began reading out loud once more "'Lincoln's private secretary, Mr. Nicolay, was at Baltimore in attendance at the Convention… and wrote a letter to Mr. Hay, who had been left in charge of the executive office in his absence, whether the President has any preference, either personal or on the score of policy; or whether he wishes not even to interfere by a confidential intimation… Please get this information for me, if possible.'"

Zack interrupted, "Wait, dudes, does anyone else find this a bit weird that you, Colonel Hay and your buddy Nicolay – who I never realized was *really* the senior of you two secretaries to Lincoln – referred to yourselves in the third person in your own 10 volume set?"

Rick looked at his brother and gave a vertical chopping motion with his hand. Zack quieted down. The rest of us looked at Zack, thinking about the slight, but important, point he made. Hay responded with a blank face and then motioned to Louise to keep reading. At least Hay didn't throw a roundhouse punch at Zack – which would have probably cleared the audience of 1904 busy-bodies who were intent on eavesdropping with their slightly twisted bodies and enormously "big ears."

Louise picked up where she left off, reading out loud, "'The letter was shown to the President, who endorsed upon it this memorandum: 'Wish not to interfere about V.P. Can not interfere about platform. Convention must judge for itself.' This positive and final instruction was sent at once to Mr. Nicolay, and by him communicated to the President's most intimate friends in the Convention. It is altogether probable that the ticket of 1864 would have been nominated without a contest had it not been for (this) general impression (from Lincoln).'"

Zack looked at Louise, Rick and then at John Hay, "Are you telling me that President Lincoln ditched his completely loyal and faithful Vice President, Hannibal Hamlin, as an after-thought because he didn't want to piss off the GOP convention hacks over whom he had complete control? No way, Hay, no way. That makes no sense at all!"

Putzi, who had been noticeably quiet up to now, leaned forward and growled something in German that I did not understand but clearly John Hay did. Hay leered at Putzi, then dropped his head. Silence descended on us all.

Rick, seeming to understand Putzi's intent, broke the silence. "Colonel Hay, I have a question for you."

Hay, whose composure was looking more and more downtrodden, barely lifted his head and nodded an acceptance to Rick's question.

24

Forging History

1904 The Grand Hotel, Michigan

Rick continued, "You had a history of writing letters on behalf of the President, did you not?"

Hay squeaked out an almost unintelligible "Yes I did."

Rick reached over to the table and picked up something. From a file full of documents, Rick pulled up a printed sheet of paper and began reading,

> "'*Washington, Nov. 21, 1864. Dear Madam–*
>
> *I have been shown in the files of the War Department a statement of the Adjutant General of Massachusetts that you are the mother of five sons who have died gloriously on the field of battle.*
>
> *I feel how weak and fruitless must be any word of mine which should attempt to beguile you from the grief of a loss so overwhelming. But I cannot refrain from tendering you the consolation that may be found in the thanks of the Republic they died to save.*

I pray that our Heavenly Father may assuage the anguish of your bereavement, and leave you only the cherished memory of the loved and lost, and the solemn pride that must be yours to have laid so costly a sacrifice upon the altar of freedom.

Yours, very sincerely and respectfully,
Lincoln

Louise began unexpectedly crying, in response to this letter from Lincoln. Putzi, though angry in his German words to Hay, had been stoic in his remaining silence began to tear up, too. The letter's contents were almost too hard to bear, even over a century and a half later. *Five sons lost in battle.*

Rick, waited until the emotion began to abate. He took a breath, a deeper breath than usual and continued, "In fact, Lincoln never wrote those words, did he?" He paused, then slowly continued, "You wrote the letter to Mrs. Bixby on behalf of the Union cause, didn't you?"

"No, the President wrote that!" He paused again, then reacted. "You have no proof to the contrary!"

Rick swayed his head side to side, preparing to play the card that a century-and-a-half of research would provide for him.

"Yes, I do have proof. Lincoln didn't write it. History has a way of catching up with lies, liars… and douche bags, Colonel Hay. President Lincoln wrote many wonderful and touching letters and speeches, to be sure. But he never wrote that. *You did.*" Proud of his brother, Zack looked at John Hay and said, "Dude it was you who wrote Saving Private Ryan's letter."

Everyone's head turned toward Zack, with a look of bewilderment.

Rick simply shook his own head… and then moved in for the kill shot, "You see, in the future, in 2017, a team of forensic linguistic researchers arrived at the truth. In a paper submitted to Digital Scholarship in the Humanities, they used a technique they developed called "n-gram tracing", to arrive at the complete conclusion that John Hay – you – wrote that letter not Abraham Lincoln and since there is no original copy available for penmanship comparisons, these clear analytics had to be relied upon. And science proved you a deceiver. It took 150 years to find the truth. And Colonel Hay, we are *from* that future. By the way, Mrs. Bixby lost two sons, not five. Maybe at the time, you did not know the exact number…"

Louise jumped back in, "If you lied in November of 1864 about Lincoln writing this Bixby letter, most-surely you had the capacity to lie in other letters, umm, in another specific letter, uhhh, that Convention letter to John Nicolay, written earlier in July of that same *election* year, when you penned those *supposed* non-committal comments from President Lincoln, eliminating Vice President Hannibal Hamlin from the reelection ticket, didn't you?"

Like a volcano erupting from a mountain, Hay burst from dormant defensiveness into an anguished cry as his head fell into his open palms and years of burning guilt began to escape from him. His cry changed to moans. His body shook.

Doc and I did not react, we allowed the *lava* to find its own path. The busybodies harrumphed and picked up their sunshade umbrellas, adjusted their wide-brimmed (and bowler) hats and exited.

John Hay, former Private Secretary to President Abraham Lincoln, breveted Civil War Union Army officer, former U.S. Ambassador to the Court of Sr. James in England and 37th Secretary of State under two Presidents was reduced to deep sobs as the truth of what he had done to Hannibal Hamlin and *thus* what he had allowed to be done to the entire plight of African slaves in America. Lying for decades, this moment overwhelmed him.

Sobbing, he said, "Yes, I wrote that letter to Mrs. Bixby; and yes, for political reasons… I betrayed a good man who should have continued on as Vice President… And because Hamlin did not ascend to the Presidency, I also sentenced all black former slaves to a different type of slavery – the horrible conditions… of Andrew Johnson's reconstruction period." He paused, "I was a bastard, an arrogant, manipulative young bastard."

Hay wept even more; the cries of this man transitioned from those of a pent-up liar, remorseful only for being caught, to a man responsible for the horrible fate of one third of his countrymen – anguished blacks, destined for a continued slavery of another sort along with their progeny.

His crying was inconsolable. We felt his sadness so deeply. It was impossible not to.

Zack and Rick, quietly walked over to John Hay; they bent over him and draped their arms around Hay in a combined embrace.

Hay's sobbing shoulders soon relaxed and as calm returned to him. His groans ceased.

Then, with a twinkle in his eye, Zack said to Hay, for all of us to hear, "Well, at least we all understood the common use of the word "bastard".

Section VI

25

Preparing to Save Lincoln

1863 Washington D. C.

The speed at which things accelerated was incredible.

We worked late into the night preparing how to best travel by spacetime on Telluric Current One from Mackinac Island in 1904 to July of 1863 in Washington D.C. We determined what we must first do as a team, just months after what most people consider to be the historical success for the Union at Gettysburg. Hay fully understood the truth that the battle was *not* a success, at least not a *total* success. His information for us was so deeply valuable. Hay told us that President Lincoln ran the war by telegraph from the War Department, just down the street from both the White House *and* the Willard Hotel.

During the Battle of Gettysburg, the telegraph line between the headquarters of commanding officer General Meade and President Lincoln's War Department was completely sabotaged and Lincoln sat for three days during the Battle of Gettysburg not knowing what was going on. It had to be sheer terror for him.

In our discussions, Hay stated it this way: "We had every chance in the world of capturing General Robert E. Lee at the end of that third day of fighting. The Union Army trapped Lee's forces against the Potomac River; the rebels had no bridges over which to cross. They had all been destroyed. Then, Gen. George Meade made the oddest decision – he took a rest – he literally stopped pursuing Lee for days so that his own soldiers could recover. It was insane!"

The anger with which John Hay spoke was every bit real. As a young man in 1863 Hay was there at Gettysburg on the 3rd day of the colossal fight between the Union and Confederated forces and he observed Meade's foolish actions.

"Gen. John Sedgewick, and Brig. General George Custer had both fought hard and gained positive national attention at Gettysburg." Hay said, "But it was Gen. Meade who failed our country by failing to finish the job of annihilating Lee's troops. It was inexcusable! They were in our hands… and then, over a period of days as Meade's troops rested, Lee's troops eventually and covertly constructed make-shift bridges and crossed the swollen Potomac River on those bridges on July 13th. The war could have ended the very last *new* day of the battle, July 4th, 1863. Had that happened, there would be no General Grant at Appomattox and therefore no President Grant in the future. Instead, General Sedgewick and General Custer would have been the future hero-Presidents rather than Grant. Two more years of continued death and destruction, would NOT have happened since the Civil War would have ended in July of 1863 rather than April of 1865."

Putzi innocently asked Hay, "What did General Grant and General Custer do?"

Hay responded, "I said *no Grant at Appomattox* for the surrender of Confederate General Robert E. Lee."

Putzi, confused but undeterred continued to prod with a slight air of defensiveness, "I understood what you meant. My question is 'What did Grant do at Gettysburg that upset you?"

Hay responded, "Grant did nothing!"

Putzi continued, "Then why didn't Grant reprimand Meade and take over the battle, pressing it to the bitter end, capturing or killing Lee on the last day of the Battle of Gettysburg?"

Hay looked confused. "I told you he did nothing, because he could not! He wasn't there." He paused, "Custer was there. Sedgewick was there and they could have been the heroes on that day with Calvary troops brutally attacking Lee and others on the banks of the Potomac River on July 4th and ending the Civil War by capturing or killing Lee and his general staff."

Putzi, Louise and Doc all looked surprised at both the Grant comment and Hay's awareness of what Custer and Sedgewick could have done.

"What?" Putzi said, on behalf of them all. "General Ulysses Grant did not fight at Gettysburg?"

Hay, dismissed them with a firm wave of his hand, "What *are* you people? Do you not even know American Civil War military history?" The arrogant John Hay had returned, it seemed. We just looked at him. We stared back at him, disappointed at his response.

Jack Lewis looked at John Hay and simply said, "Settle down, Colonel." Hay realized how prideful, rude and dismissive he sounded; and regained his composure in both his tone and intensity. He glanced at Rick Besso, who had kept quiet during this exchange. They exchanged knowing glances.

Hay said, "Rick, you're a West Pointer, like Grant, Custer, Sedgewick and Lee. Why was Grant not at Gettysburg and why was July 1-3, 1863 so important to the Civil War and could have been even more important to the nation – both then and now?"

26

Meade and Gettysburg

1863

Rick nodded his head and stood up prepared, as if to give a military briefing.

He looked around and began, "Friends, Grant was not there to help Meade because Grant was leading the Battle of Vicksburg on July 3rd – also on that same day, the battle of Fort Hudson and Helena, Arkansas was successfully concluded by other Union generals. On this particular day in 1863 the South was divided in half and Grant felt that for all intents and purposes, the war of the rebellion was guaranteed to be quickly over. But he was premature in his belief – two years premature, at the cost of hundreds of thousands of additional young men who died, from both the North and the South."

The pause was profound.

Hay took over for Rick with a deep sadness in his voice, "The Confederate general, Robert E. Lee, escaped failure. In fact, The

Tycoon wrote something brutal to Meade ten days later on July 14th 1863 when he learned of the commanding general's failure and Lee's escape."

We let Hay continue speaking with an authority known only to a select few men who had lived through those first three hot and bloody days of July, 1863.

From memory Hay spoke Lincoln's written words to Meade, "I do not believe you appreciate the magnitude of the misfortune involved in Lee's escape – He was within your easy grasp, and to have closed upon him would, in connection with our other late successes, have ended the war–As it is, the war will be prolonged indefinitely." Hay paused and then continued reciting Lincoln's written words, "Your golden opportunity is gone, and I am distressed immeasurably because of it—".

We sat silent. Hay then continued speaking to us, "The Tycoon never sent that letter, though he signed it, sitting at his desk in the War Department next to the telegraph." He paused again and looked at the floor and then touched his suitcoat pocket, "I have that letter on me; I always carry it in my billfold, as a reminder to myself to finish what I begin."

Doc and I looked at each other. "When was it dated?" we both asked at the same time.

Hay withdrew the folded and faded letter in a leathery billfold-like case, opened it up and matter-of-factly read the date, "July 14th, 1863."

Doc looked at John Hay and said with somewhat bridled energy, "Colonel Hay, that's our pass through the enemy's lines of history to re-meet President Lincoln and save his life."

Hay jumped to his feet. His expression of genuine surprise made all of us smile. "By Jove, it is!" He grabbed a half-filled glass of wine from the table and proposed a toast. We joined him with whatever un-corked liquid in our individual possession. "To saving The Tycoon!" he offered. We repeated this brief and powerful toast. It only seemed fitting and proper to have a celebration dinner. And that we soon did.

We now had the "how and when" to return to Lincoln in 1863 and save him while ending his political career; what we still needed were the deeper details.

As we adjourned to the elegant Main Dining Room of the Grand Hotel to enjoy a wonderfully prepared delicious meal, we were each ready and willing to go change history – for the better. Our discussion in the Main Dining room at the Grand Hotel on Mackinac Island, Michigan was a rich combination of laughter, gratitude and enjoyment of the moment. We spent a couple hours asking Hay to tell us stories about his time as Lincoln's Secretary – and of his time living in the White House. The Lincoln stories brought us great laughter. Story after story of Lincoln the Illinois lawyer, then candidate for President and then as The Tycoon.

After dinner we all returned to John Hay's room. We reviewed lists of historical moments, personal items, political people and their personal motives that could possibly work to get the impeachment and conviction of Abraham Lincoln to occur in the sweltering summer months of 1863.

With the benefit of history being in our rearview mirror, the obvious seemed to leap out: Lincoln's suspension of habeas corpus, the arrest of Rep. Clement Vallandigham, Lincoln's General War Order No. 1, his firing on fellow citizens. We discussed these and more. Historian and future Idaho Lt. Governor, David Leroy's seminal work aided us greatly. We talked about elected officials who could initiate the President's removal. The options and possibilities were so numerous that they began to overwhelm us.

Then I asked, "Friends, what about approaching this problem from a different perspective?"

Doc said, "Continue..."

I answered, "What about taking what we have in our hands – the information on Hamlin – and dealing directly with him?"

"With whom?" asked Jack.

"Han Hamlin…the Vice President?" Hay responded, the very idea catching him by a desired surprise.

Doc asked, "By bringing him into our little band of spacetime travelers, as we did before with Mark Twain…and with you, Colonel and with you, Jack?"

"Exactly," I responded. They looked at me as I pulled a very slight two volume set of old books from my satchel. The set was entitled The Life and Times of Hannibal Hamlin.

I nodded to Doc and John Hay. "I thought we might need some additional background intel on Vice President Hamlin as we'd soon be planning how we could *best* go back through spacetime and help President Lincoln," I said.

I nodded to Zack and Rick, "Is it ok for me *to spill the beans*?"

Both brothers laughed. "Sure, go ahead."

John Hay looked up, "What? We didn't have beans for dinner. And if we *did*, why would you want to spill perfectly good food on the table or the floor?"

That's when both brothers howled, "Here we go again…"

John Hay was lost, so I just continued. "You'll get the meaning of it here in a second."

Hay nodded a sort of 1904 linguistic acceptance to yet another odd phrase that wouldn't be commonly used until 1919.

I continued, "Earlier, I directed the Besso Brothers to go to the Yale Library, when they went to help save your son's life – and check out this two-volume set on Hannibal Hamlin's life. I knew we would need more information."

Zack laughed and responded, "Yeah, we used Del's college library card! I wonder what the fees are going to be when we return the books!"

We all laughed.

I opened up the cover to Hannibal Hamlin's biography.

"Published in 1899. Penciled by some anonymous hand from the past are these words: *History always overtakes untruth.*"

A relieved John Hay responded, "Maybe so."

Then, he looked at our group, "Consider the beans as having been spilled."

Zack howled.

27

Piecing Together History

1863 Washington D. C.

Sitting in John Hay's room at the Grand Hotel taking our turns, reading out loud T*he Life and Times of Hannibal Hamlin* made for a wonderfully refreshing afternoon. It's hard to explain, except that the author captured a part of American history that both included eyewitness testimony of hard/true facts… and it included grace.

For us, the book was life-giving. Written by the former Vice President's grandson, Charles E. Hamlin, thirty-five years after Lincoln's first Vice President was rejected from the ticket, the two volumes are respectful in tone, accurate in facts and forgiving in nature. Listening to the words as they were read out loud, by *each* of us, captivated *all* of us, Hay especially. Jack Lewis's Irish accent gave a wonderfully light sense to so many of the chapters. He seemed to thoroughly enjoy reading the stories out loud to us.

Putzi remarked, "You truly are a wonderful story teller, Jack. Have you ever thought of writing stories that could be read aloud to others?"

Zack couldn't help himself, "I wish we had the Internet; in the future I'd just look at you right now and say "Google it!"

Putzi wrinkled his forehead with strained eyes and responded. "Doodle it?"

We all just looked at Putzi, shook our heads and refocused on Jack as he finished that particular chapter.

During a brief transition as the book was passed to him for his portion of the recital, Hay looked down at the two-volume set and said to us, "Before he published this set in 1899, the author sent me an early draft manuscript. As I read the manuscript, I was struck by an expression he often used – that his grandfather had been *retired* from the Vice Presidency." Hay paused, "What a strange and yet, kind, way of referring to his forced exit from the presidential ticket *and* ultimately from the Presidency, once The Tycoon was assassinated." He paused again, then said repeated, as if only to himself, "*Retired*."

Hay opened the book, looking for something near the back of the book, "I gave a short review of the manuscript prior to publication, which he included somewhere at the end of his book."

"Here it is," Hay mumbled as he found it, tapping it with his right index finger. "Nothing much, really. Nicolay was quite in-depth in his response as he provided Hamlin's grandson with detailed observations and corrections, including some additions provided regarding Vice President Hamlin's son, General Hamlin – who was the author's father."

Rather than turning back to the queued-up section to continue the reading, John Hay put on his spectacles and read out loud his own printed note in the back of the book. Something was happening. We all felt it.

"Dear Mr. Hamlin,

I have your letter of February 20th, 1898. Mr. Nicolay has made so full and complete a statement of all the matters referring to your father's intimate relations with President Lincoln, and to

Mr. Lincoln's wish for your father's renomination, that it seems altogether unnecessary for me to write anything additional..."

Hay put down the book and looked at us. Then he directed us to listen as he returned to the place and continued reading, "Here's the *concluding* sentence, 'I believe (Nicolay) to be absolutely correct in his statement of these matters of which I was *not* personally cognizant.'" This time he looked directly into our faces and said, "That's me talking...I knew what I'd done. I *was* cognizant of my lie, my deceit in sending the false note to Nicolay, counterfeiting Lincoln's handwriting so that the GOP Convention would choose another running mate for the President, rather than simply accepting the incumbent Vice President. My own manipulative actions threw open the whole convention and eliminated the chance for a good man to remain in the Vice Presidency. I lied to John Nicolay, I lied to Hannibal Hamlin, I lied to Hamlin's son, the general, I lied to his grandson, the author, and I lied to Abraham Lincoln."

His eyes became weepy.

"I am done covering up the lies." He paused.

"Dear friends, we don't need to read any further. I know what we have to do. It's not the convention of 1864 nor the assassination of 1865 that we must address and stop. We have to return to 1863, with these two books by Hamlin's grandson and show them to Hannibal Hamlin. I must admit to him that in his near future of 1864, the younger version of me, John Hay, will attempt to unjustly treat him – and that we are there to make things right. Louise, your suggestion that we pursue impeachment and conviction is what we should do, even with all the complexity that involves. And we need to tell this to Vice President Hamlin, whether he'll initially understand it or not. Are we all in agreement?"

As the last hold-out, I signaled that we were now in 100% agreement.

Pushing aside loose papers and grabbing an inkwell and pen, John Hay was crystal clear in his convictions and each of us followed him. Hay said, "Now, let's prepare the argument for impeachment and conviction of Abraham Lincoln."

The hours stretched on. Finally, the team came to a conclusion using the notes they had from David Leroy. Rick Besso began the finishing touches on the team's approach to Impeaching and Convicting Lincoln. Ice tea and small cakes were set about the room, as each of us busied ourselves.

Addressing us in Hay's hotel suite, Rick said, "Historians have argued that President Lincoln abused the power of the Presidency on numerous occasions and in various ways, making himself vulnerable to articles of impeachment by the House, conviction by the Senate and removal from office. Their arguments fall short when contrasted with Lincoln's extraordinary courage, and yet, questionable executive behavior. It was an era of extraordinary violent and rebellious events facing him. Lincoln often expressed that his sole goal was to save the Union, no matter what."

Rick paused and took a sip of tea and then continued, "Anecdotal examples of this abuse of power range from his suspension of habeas corpus early in the Civil War to arrest and indefinitely jail political opponents with no set trial date. In the case of the sitting Ohio U.S. Congressman, Clement Vallandigham, who was arrested and imprisoned for a significant period of time, the uproar was huge. By direct order of President Lincoln, Vallandigham was eventually released and then unceremoniously deposited behind enemy lines to the Confederacy. The Union "Peace Democrats" (who were known as the Copperheads, because of their vicious viper-like attacks against their Union opponents in Congress) were furious for losing Vallandigham to the South; the Radical Republicans and Abolitionists were equally furious at Lincoln for releasing such a traitor. Lincoln was hated by the Confederacy, the Copperheads *and* the Radical Republicans."

Rick looked at the group of us and said, "Even with all that vitriol against the President, these issues increased the anger of congressmen and senators but not the anger of the citizens. The nation was still with Lincoln. The Civil War was two years old and war fatigue was starting to grow, but not a lot. To press that emotional edge and move public opinion, the only thing we can do to make the case to the people of the United States is to show that President Lincoln failed to bring the war to its natural end at Gettysburg, when Meade let Lee slip away into the night. And for that terrible failure, all confidence in the President could become eroded. The combined forces of the Copperhead Democrats and the Radical Republicans would then stop Lincoln by impeachment and conviction. We just need a leader to fan the flames."

I said, "Han Hamlin?"

Louise responded, "He is the logical leader with his credentials; and he is directly in line to assume the Presidency."

Rick looked directly at John Hay, "I know you want to *see* The Tycoon, but what you really want to do is *save* him, correct?"

Hay nodded *yes*.

Rick continued, "So, who we really need to *see* is the *Vice* President. We need to see him in Washington D. C. on July 14th, 1863... the day Mr. Lincoln signed that letter to General Meade. We need to bring your book, volumes nine and ten, as well as the VP's biography by Hamlin's grandson. And we need to do it now."

We gathered up all the documents and books, placed them in our satchels and walked down to the shoreline of Lake Huron at the base of the Grand Hotel on Mackinac Island, grouped together around Telluric Current One. Along with John Hay, we placed our fingers on the signature of A. Lincoln and in an instant, all of us were gone."

Section VII

28

Han Hamlin

1863 Washington D. C.

Hannibal Hamlin first ran for U. S. Congress as a Democrat in 1840. He lost to the Whig Party nominee, Elisha Allen, but challenged him two years later and won. Hamlin came to Washington D. C. in 1843 as a Democrat Member of the House of Representatives from Maine. He was known as *Han* to his friends. And also, to his *opponents* – he had no enemies.

In 1846 this ambitious young Congressman wanted to become a U.S. Senator, but just as he had been defeated for the House of Representatives on his first try, he was rejected for the Senate seat as well. A year later the incumbent Senator unfortunately died during a knee operation. Hamlin was selected to fill that seat.

Ups and downs, opportunities and failures, yet timing seemed ultimately always in Han Hamlin's favor.

As a Democrat, he served as a U.S. Senator until 1857, when he was elected Governor of Maine as a Republican. He resigned from the Senate and he resigned from the Democrat Party due to their stand in favor of slavery; he served for only one month as Governor. It was a part of a larger plan developed by the fledgling new political Republican Party. He resigned as Governor and was immediately re-appointed by the new Maine GOP Legislature to the U.S. Senate as a Republican. By 1860 he was a well-respected leader of this newly formed political party. So much so, that during the 1860 presidential convention in Chicago, Hamlin proved his national leadership skills for the party and was rewarded by being nominated as Lincoln's running mate.

His response was honest and would represent his entire political resume – a biography of chance, loss, opportunity and grace. He said the following in his acceptance speech: "Unsolicited, unexpected and undesired, the nomination has been conferred upon me. Unsolicited as it was, I accept it."

Four years later he was *unexpectedly* retired as Vice President. His time *in the sun*, it seemed, was over.

And it was our team's goal to ensure one final unsolicited, unexpected, yet probably desired opportunity would come his way as the 17th President of the United States of America. And Abe Lincoln would live to see it. Such was our lofty plan as we felt the swoosh of time and space pass us by, landing our band of travelers in 1863, within wartime Washington D.C. We had in our possession Lincoln's letter to General Meade. John Hay took lead, along with Doc, Louise, Jack, Putzi, Rick, Zack and me following him.

Rick's *love* of studying history was interesting to watch in comparison to Hay's first-person experience of *living* history.

Rick said, "Hey, Hamlin sometimes boarded at the St. Charles Hotel at 3rd and Pennsylvania. I say we should head over there," and moved towards the left from the War Department building, where Lincoln obviously sat and wrote the letter to Meade.

Hay shook his head, *no*. We all stopped in our tracks. He mumbled to Rick while turning to the right and heading in the opposite direction toward the White House, "You'd be correct if we were at the start of the Rebellion in 1860 or early '61. But not in July of 1863. The St. Charles Hotel was notorious for inviting slave owners in, while housing their slaves in the basement, shackled to the walls. As an abolitionist, Hamlin was disgusted and left that hotel."

Hay knew instinctively where Vice President Hamlin would be found. Down the street from the White House – at the Willard Hotel, 1401 Pennsylvania Avenue. He even remembered the specific hotel room number.

We arrived at this luxurious hotel. The bulk of our group stayed in the lobby. Doc motioned for me to assist Hay on this leg of the journey.

So, Hay and I went to Hamlin's door. He knocked in a unique way. He tapped the door once then paused and tapped twice more, and whispered "Stop that knocking at the door.... "As he looked at me, he added with a smile, "Even my knock on the door sounds familiar again." I had no idea what he was saying. What he whispered meant nothing to me. I looked at him, confused and countered with "How about seven knocks with 'Shave and a haircut, two bits?'"

He had no idea what *I* was talking about. I'd forgotten that *that* knock wasn't around in 1863. Life's little 'dailynesses' seem to just happen and change without notice.

29

The Conversation

1863 Washington D. C.

Hay's knock brought gentle, deliberate footfalls on the other side of the hotel door. The opening of the lock occurred and the door swung slowly open. There, face to face with John Hay and me, was Vice President of the United States Hannibal 'Han' Hamlin.

Hay spoke first, "Mr. Vice President, it's been a *very* long time since we last saw one another."

An awkward pause followed, then a movement of Hamlin's facial muscles and his right eyebrow, as he squinted, searching his memory to see who this visitor was. Hamlin shifted his feet only slightly, leaned a bit on the door jam and then gathering himself, looked keenly into Hay's face. "Yes, I believe it has been. You are Dr. Charles Hay, father of young John Hay, one of President Lincoln's 'Boys', are you not?" He continued while opening up the door and inviting us in, "Your son is quite a decent young man. He'll go places in life. He's an honest fellow."

Hay winced, if only to himself, then smiled and said as Hamlin invited us in. Hay introduced me, "This is my traveling partner, Mr. Will Clark."

Hamlin acknowledged my presence with a nod and continued, "Now, how may I help you, gentleme*n*? Surely you have greater access to The White House than even I, as a result of your son?"

Hay responded as he walked into the room and motioned me to stay the doorway, "It's actually about how I may be able to help *you*."

Hay looked at me with eyes that seemed to say 'I've got this' as he continued to motion for me to stay outside and guard the door. I obeyed.

As the door shut behind the two men, I heard the bolt on the door latch close. I was left in the hallway to ensure no one interrupted the conversation within room 277. From the end of the hallway, I retrieved a wooden chair and propped it against the hotel room door and leaned back in it, both ensuring no interruptions and yet *hopeful* of possible eavesdropping.

I heard nothing.

Diplomatic gentlemen tend to speak in tones, low and directly proportionate to the large and serious nature that huge historical occasions demand.

I thought to myself, 'Their whispers say it all…

Geoffrey Chaucer once wrote, "Time and tide wait for no man." In 1863 at the Willard Hotel in Washington D.C. *I* waited on time, believing that the tide of history *could* wait. I sat outside of the Vice President's hotel room for five hours, unsuccessfully trying to hear snippets of conversation. Hunger drove me to the Willard lobby to seek food and reconnect with my team. I left a hand-written note in pencil stuck in the Vice President's door frame, '2 pm. Went for food. Will return soon.'

Zack Besso said it best as he stood in the downstairs lobby and greeted me as I approached the group, "Dude, between waiting for hours in the Grand Hotel lobby and now the Willard lobby, each of us has become a type of political 'lobbyist'… get it?"

I couldn't waste the moment. Pointing to the floor, as I walked toward the group, and with a couple dramatic jabs of my right index finger, I said, "Yep, Zack, this very floor is, *shall we say*, the source of un-holy ground in politics." I looked at Doc, remembering his use of similar dramatics when he opened my eyes at Café Central in Vienna. The spacetime travelling team looked at me quizzically. I continued, "This very lobby of the Willard Hotel birthed the myth for the term *lobbyist*. It seems U. S. Grant enjoyed whiskey and cigars at the Willard when he was President. Courtiers from business and industry often joined him in this lobby to smoke, imbibe and discuss legislation." I paused, "But…"

Putzi smiled and finished my story, "Ja, that was the origin of the myth – and maybe President Grant *did* do that, but the term goes back to Europe in the early 1640's from England's House of Commons and the several lobbies that are found surrounding Parliament." He took a draw from his most recent cigar and slowly blew the smoke into the air above them all. "We had the same thing in Germany, during the Weimar Republic."

"Correct on all counts, Putzi," Jack responded, as he lit up his pipe. "I suppose I could find some medieval equivalents of these types of political animals…'

Then without missing a beat, Putzi nodded to Jack and then asked Rick, "In the spirit of President Grant and whiskey, do you happen to have any of your West Point friend's Blackened American Whiskey on you? You know the stuff through which Metallurgy blasts their Bingo-inspired music?"

Rick's brother, Zack laughed, "You mean how my West Point classmate Dave Pickerel and Metallica use their 'Black Noise' in distilling whiskey – and it's Ringo, not Bingo, Herr Stutzi…" Zack paused, "… yet, I will say that Metallica's drummer, Lars Ulrich, has indeed been called the Ringo Starr of heavy metal music…" Zack looked at me, then he looked at Rick and slowly said, "Lars knows how to… *ride the lightning.*"

Putzi responded, "Is this where, in the future, I'll be able to say "*Poodle this*?"

Rick laughed, "It's actually "*'Google this.'* But yes, you're close."

He had a fifth of Blackened whiskey in his own hand-tote. He smiled and unveiled it to us. Indeed, *time and tide wait for no man*; as Rick opened it, we could all hear the Tuesday bells in the capitol city ringing; it was 2pm. He handed out the crystal glasses. Zack sang, "Time marches on for whom the bell tolls."

Metallica and Ernest Hemingway apparently had more than just one thing in common with each other *and* U.S. Grant. If the Willard Hotel lobby was good enough for Abraham Lincoln and Ulysses S. Grant, it was also good enough for our weary band of travelers celebrating the "future memory" of Dave Pickerel and Metallica's open bottle of Blackened whiskey.

They sipped, rested and waited in the lobby.

I grabbed a plate of food from the newfangled thing called a *buffet* and sat with my friends enjoying the assortment of Civil War era foods. I returned after a short bit, to the Vice President's hallway, sitting once again in the chair slightly propped up against the door. I hoped that the many hours it had been since John Hay shook hands with Hannibal Hamlin had been successful. I'd soon find out.

The door opened slightly, jarring me suddenly. I stood to my feet and set aside the wooden chair. John Hay peered through the doorway and motioned me in to join them. As I stepped over the threshold, I saw the Vice President of the United States slumped forward in a chair with his head in his hands, quietly saying "How can this be?"

30

O.K.

1863 Washington D. C.

Clearly, in the course of the many hours they'd been together John Hay had used the books we'd brought to successfully communicate to Han Hamlin the truths of spacetime travel, of his own experience with having us save the life of his son in the future and of the future of the country. I sat ready, just outside their door, in case Hay needed me to further explain any of the spacetime complexities. He apparently did a fine job; I was unneeded at that point.

The shock of Lincoln's future assassination seemed to overwhelm Hamlin – much more than the reality that he would be jettisoned from the Vice Presidency.

Entering in to join them, I sat down in an adjacent seat, about two feet from Hamlin and unconsciously placed my hand on his shoulder. It was close quarters; I suppose I must have thought it only natural to take this informal liberty. I'm not sure.

Hamlin lifted his head from his hands and began to pour out his reactions to both of us.

"My professional training was in law, not science. I live in the world of words and law, of service and of loyalty." He paused, "Not in the world of Newtonian physics and hard-edged seasons of time travel and such…"

I responded, "Begging your pardon, Mr. Vice President, that's not the whole truth."

He jerked his head toward me, "What are you saying, Mr. Clark?'

"I'm saying that before you lived in law, politics and elected office, you were a farmer, correct?"

"Yes, that's correct, my father's Last Will and Testament forced me to stay on our family farm to take care of my mother until I was 21 years of age. I certainly didn't want it that way."

I responded, "And during those early years you lived by the natural science of watching the weather patterns, understanding the seasons, seeing livestock be born, grow and be harvested, correct?"

"Yes, that's what farmers do."

I continued speaking as I leaned in toward him, just inches away from his face, "Han, we need you to return in your mind to your days as a farmer and look at what we're now facing, as if it was a *storm-after-storm* weather front coming your way. It is time for all of us to protect 'the farm', protect the crops, protect the livestock and protect the lives of our families and friends through an organized, scientific way." I paused, "We need you to put your hand to the plow and not look back. Do you understand that?"

Hamlin listened and seemed to take it all in.

He looked up at the ceiling as if recalling something of interest and then slowly responded, "We have an expression in Massachusetts and Maine, where I come from, that started in '39 with The Boston Morning Post. It's a simple local expression. Then, when Van Buren ran for President, he made it nationally known." Hamlin paused, "It's a strange one, and it's probably not used in your day – in the future."

I listened, expecting another one of those strange 19th century words or phrases.

He continued, "Anyway, the term is *O.K.*"

Han paused, taking measure of us receiving the word and then continued. "It means all is correct. *I'm O. K. with you...* and what you need to do." He paused once again and then lowered his voice, "We need to remember Mr. Shakespeare's admonition, which is most appropriate at this very minute, given what we're about to do to our national government, 'Discretion is the better part of valor.' This is where *you* would say, as *we* say in 1863 – *O.K.*"

I laughed and no longer worried if Hamlin had it in himself to demand that Meade attack and win the day at Gettysburg. *He did!* Hamlin would need to use Telluric Current One to return with John and me from July 14th, 1863 to the *new* last day of the battle, July 4th, 1863 and take command of the final day of the Battle of Gettysburg. The remaining ones in our group would have to stay in Washington D. C. "*O.K.* Mr. Vice President, we are of one mind," John Hay said as he ended their marathon session in the Willard Hotel. "Shall we now go down to the lobby and meet the rest of our team?" As if on cue all three of us smiled at each other and said at the same time…"*O.K.!*

31

We Touch the Future-Past

1863 Washington D. C.

After we finished our time of introductions between the Vice President and our group, all of us shared a dinner meal at the Willard's lovely restaurant.

We agreed to regroup in two hours, thus allowing Hamlin to find the needed documents with signatures from 10 days previous, during the Battle of Gettysburg.

With those documents' signatures and DNA, some of our group would travel to July 3rd, 1863 to initiate the needed parts of the plan. The others would remain in Washington D.C. on July 14th, 1863.

During the next two hours, Doc, Louise, the Colonel and I went on a walk past the White House towards the War Department. Putzi, Jack Lewis and the Besso Brothers set their clocks for two hours and walked in the opposite direction towards Capitol Hill.

As we approached the corner of the White House grounds, I was first to speak. "John, how in the world did you talk Hamlin into joining us?"

Hay responded, "I didn't. I ultimately let his grandson's writing 'talk to him'".

Louise said, "Wait, you simply gave him the book that his grandson Charles Eugene Hamlin published roughly thirty years from now? That's it?"

Hay looked at her and then at us, "How many of our team have children, young or adult?"

Doc reacted, "What's that got to do with it?"

Hay stopped us, like so many tourists have done for decades and decades, standing outside of the North Portico entrance to the Executive Mansion. I felt like I needed my iPhone to grab a selfie with everyone, but then shook off the misplaced idea.

Hay continued with intense emotion, "Each of you saw the incredible joy at seeing the return of my dead son, did you not? My son was dead yet he came back to life."

We all nodded.

"Imagine for just a second that an adult child we loved was off at war, like Hamlin was experiencing with his son, Charles, leading troops on the side of the Union. Lists of dead Union soldiers and officers were posted every day. No family was immune. The Vice President in 1863 – *today* – had no knowledge of what the future held for his son."

Something caught Hay's attention. He looked up and pointed to the front of the Executive Mansion, to a window in the top right front. "That's my room, well mine and John Nicolay's." He stood there like a statue examining the front of the President's House, without saying a word. Then, he motioned us on, towards the War Department building. We followed his lead, each of us looking back like rubber-necking D. C. tourists ... only for us, it was stretching back a century and a half to look at Lincoln's White House.

He returned to his earlier thought, "…He had no knowledge of what the future held for his son. He'd obviously seen his son, the General, at Gettysburg near Meade's tent, but he had great fear of what was on the horizon for his son's life, as the war would surely drag on. And here I came into the suite at the Willard with a book, published in the future by his son's son. The grandson *couldn't* have come into existence if his father had been killed in combat. The mere presence of the book – and the author's preface brought Hamlin to tears. It read something like, 'I am chiefly indebted to my father, General Charles Hamlin, my grandfather's right-hand man for many years.' And it was only then, that I told him I was John Hay and *not* my father, whom he originally thought I was. *We both sat down quickly.* My own head was spinning and I was worried that his world would collapse. It didn't. Nor did our discussion end."

Louise prodded him, "Did you tell him of your own son and how the Besso Brothers were used to save his life?"

"I did," he responded. "I told him of what I had experienced in losing my son in the prime of his life."

The Colonel teared up, stopped walking once more and then looked up into the sky. "I told him that you were all gifts of God to me. The Vice President followed up with this: 'Apparently, you and your friends are all gifts of God to me, to my family, too."

"It was at that point that, as we sat in the Willard Hotel's comfortable chairs, I introduced him to dog-eared pages of his grandson's biography. And he dutifully turned to each one and read them out loud." He paused, "I wish that Zack Besso was with us right now, he'd have the right phrase for what I witnessed. Something about my face having been blown off my shoulders…"

"Do you mean, *'My mind was blown'*?" I asked.

"Yes, yes, that's it," Hay said. "My mind was blown! As I told him of what you had done with those tyrants in the future, in 1913, he was wide-eyed and listening. When I told of your desire to save the lives of key future U.S. Presidents, starting with Lincoln."

Doc asked, "How did he respond to the fact that he'd soon be dropped from the ticket?"

Hay responded, "He was shocked. He began to question if somehow, I was deceiving him. So, I let him read the book pages that dealt with that. And…"

John Hay choked up a bit and continued, "And… I told him of what the younger version of me would be doing against him during the next year's nominating convention. How I would falsify the note in The Tycoon's writing, and how Andrew Johnson would be the convention's choice – not him.

And that in just 41 days from when Hamlin would no longer be Vice President, that Lincoln would die at the hands of a conspiracy – and Hamlin would not be the President."

Doc asked, "What was his reaction to your admitting these things?"

"He was stoic. He looked at me, as I suppose any tight-lipped person from Maine would do and said, 'Well, that won't do, will it?"

I laughed, "Man, that's short and sweet, isn't it?"

Hay laughed, too. "*Yes, it was*. He told me that he was with us and that he deeply respected Abraham Lincoln. We began discussing the Impeachment and Conviction possibilities. Then he told me a story that was still so fresh in his mind."

Louise asked, "About what?"

Hay said, "Well, as he was telling me it, I remembered that in person I'd seen the story he was speaking about. It was in his grandson's book, so I picked up Volume 2, found the spot and began reading as he was speaking. It wasn't word for word, but it was close." We all wanted to hear what the story was.

Louise asked if Hay still had the book in his satchel, which he did. So, we stopped at the corner of Pennsylvania Avenue and the War Department, leaned against the half fence and near the trees for shade and listened as John Hay read that key section: "Mr. Hamlin arrived at Gettysburg on July 4th 1863, after the fighting had closed to find the Union lines impregnable, the enemy in retreat, and his son unharmed and recommended for promotion. President Lincoln was warning General Meade that he ought to follow up Lee lest he should escape. Mr. Hamlin reached the same conclusion and remained on the field of battle in hopes of seeing the Confederate army annihilated. One who was with Mr. Hamlin was Noah Brooks, a journalist. He later wrote, 'Here I met Vice-President Hamlin who was also a visitor at Meade's headquarters and who had been taken out to see the fight (which did not come off). As we met, Hamlin raised his hands and turned away his face with a gesture of despair… about the possible escape of the rebel army."

Doc and I looked at each other, then at John Hay. "That's why you asked the Vice President for something in writing for us to use on the Telluric Current to go back in time ten days? You want to use that moment in time to have Han Hamlin order General Meade to attack and annihilate Lee's remaining troops from Gettysburg and end the Civil War?"

People were milling about on Pennsylvania Avenue. Men were making their way from the War Department back to the Executive Mansion and vice versa.

Before Hay could respond to Doc's question, our group heard a voice cry out behind us, "Well, Mr. Charles Hay! Does *your* boy and *mine*, John, know you're in the city?"

We turned.

President Abraham Lincoln was standing in front of us.

32

Meeting Lincoln

1863 Washington D. C.

Mr. Lincoln put the palm of his left hand on John Hay's shoulder, mistaking Hay for his father. The President embraced the Colonel's right hand with a strong handshake. Standing a little to the President's left, was a beautiful young woman in her early twenties, obviously being escorted by him.

Unlike modern-day smarmy politicians, Lincoln greeted us naturally as though he had *honestly* known us a very long time; he moved away from his female guest and towards our group. He shook hands with each of us in an open two-palmed way (one clasping the hand the other covering the hand from the top) as only a warm-hearted and sincere man knows how to do, introducing himself, as if we did not know his name, "Hello, I'm Abe Lincoln and this young lady… this is Miss Elizabeth Bacon. You might have heard of her dashing fiancé, General George Custer. He's been fighting these last few days at that little town in Pennsylvania – Gettysburg." His face moved to a somber expression.

"Just last month he was promoted to the rank of Brigadier General at the age of 23, along with two other young officers! The press is calling them The Boy Generals."

He began to smile again, "Now don't that just beat all? If I was young enough, I'd appoint myself a general, too!" Lincoln scanned our faces for a response of laughter.

There was none. We just stood and looked at him, speechless. I think we all felt like one of the faces on Mount Rushmore was speaking to us. Or maybe that Disneyland's Hall of Presidents had a live host who was now in front of us. It was so extraordinarily weird.

General Custer's future bride broke the awkward silence by extending her own hand, "Please call me Libbie. It's an honor to meet you all. President Lincoln was just escorting me over to have a meal with his family."

Lincoln gushed, "This is the young woman whose future husband goes into a charge with a whoop and a shout. Well, I'm told he won't do so anymore."

Libbie assured Lincoln that he would indeed, even after they married.

"Oh, then you want to be a widow, I see," Lincoln said with a laugh.

Then he turned toward us and added, "I noticed you standing in the shade." Taking a long look at this older version of John Hay, Lincoln continued "Charles, you've grown a beard since we last saw one another. Your brother Milton had just grown a beard this year when our offices were next to each other in Springfield, before I was *arrested* and placed in that prison called The White House," he said pointing at his home.

Hay squinted his eyes, hoping that his gray hair, horvat-wrinkles and his overall increase in age would continue to protect his identity. He returned the volley, "I suppose we *all* have grown beards, Mr. President."

Lincoln guffawed and slapped Hay's back, "Well, you know how that little girl in Westfield, New York, Grace Bedell, wrote me before the Inauguration and told me I should grow my whiskers?"

Hay responded in equal good humor, "Yes, I do, sir. She was a bold and yet, sweet, little thing. The way you stooped down from the train and took her into your arms and spent time letting her feel your whiskers while you talked to her..." Hay's voice trailed off, worried for some unknown reason.

Lincoln looked at him inquisitively. "Charles, I don't remember you being on the train that day. How did you recall that special moment?"

Hay could now sense that The Tycoon was reverting to his experienced cross-examining lawyer role. It was obvious that the Colonel had a reason to worry.

Louise panicked. She pulled from her pocket a folded blank slip of crumpled paper and smiled as she said, "Mr. President, everybody in the nation read the article from the New York World! Why I even have a copy of it here.

Libbie cooed, "Oh please read it!"

Absolute fear replaced Louise's attempt at cleverness.

John Hay saw the fear in her face and acted immediately, "How ungallant of me, Louise, please allow me to read that article," he said as he placed his spectacles on the bridge of his nose, took from her the crumpled (blank) paper and began to read:

"At Westfield an interesting incident occurred. Shortly after his nomination Mr. Lincoln had received from that place a letter from a little girl, who urged him, as a means of improving his personal appearance, to wear whiskers. Mr. Lincoln at the time replied, stating that although he was obliged by the suggestion, he feared his habits of life were too fixed to admit of even so slight a change as that which letting his beard grow involved."

Hay adjusted his glasses again. Lincoln smiled broadly.

Hay continued, "Today, on reaching the place, he related the incident, and said that if that young lady was in the crowd, he should be glad to see her. There was a momentary commotion, in the midst of which an old man, struggling through the crowd, approached, leading his daughter, a girl of apparently twelve or thirteen years of age, whom he introduced to Mr. Lincoln as his Westfield correspondent."

Hay paused again and said to our little group, "Little Grace Bedell was only 11."

Lincoln nodded in agreement.

And then Hay continued, "Mr. Lincoln stooped down and kissed the child, and talked with her for some minutes. Her advice had *not* been thrown away upon the rugged chieftain. A beard of several months' growth covers (perhaps adorns) the lower part of his face. The young girl's peachy cheek must have been tickled with a stiff whisker, for the growth of which she was herself responsible."

Hay folded the paper and handed it back to Louise, who quickly returned the blank page to her purse.

Lincoln was impressed, "Why Charles, you read that like you had written it!" Lincoln looked over at Libbie and smiled.

Hay looked with a side glance at Doc and me and slowly mouthed the words. *'I did.'*

Lincoln returned his glance to us and continued, "You, your brother Milton and your son John are all reminders of my sacred time in Springfield. I cannot wait to lay this job down and return to our town and pick back up the law." He paused, "But there are now things to be done here." His face suddenly went quite serious.

"I will let *our boy*, John, know that he can take time off tonight and have dinner with you. Would you like that?"

Hay thanked the President but said, "No, Mr. President, allow me to connect with my son on my own. It's a surprise."

Lincoln signaled that he would do so and then turned to us, extended his arm to Libbie and excused himself and Miss Bacon as they walked to the Executive Mansion.

We simply all looked at one another.

John Hay broke the silence, "I guess it *does* pay, after all, to have falsely written for other people."

And I added, "*And* to have a great memory!"

We all guffawed and slumped somewhat to the grass and shrubbery line out of nervousness *and* exhilaration, at the thought of what had just happened.

33

Waiting and Touring

1863 Washington D. C.

Tourists are tourists, whether they travel across geography or travel through time. *We're all tourists.* Each of us likes to take in the sunlit landscapes, the smells of nature, the aromas of food and the sounds of a formerly distant city.

For the two groups of spacetime travelers we experienced all those things in 1863. Upon our return to the Willard Hotel, the two groups reconnected after we'd exhausted two hours of touring The Capital City, as Washingtonians called it in the 1860s. We shared observations as we regained our area in the lobby, awaiting the arrival of Han Hamlin, as promised.

Putzi kicked off the retelling of his group's visit down the long-stretching mall, heading past the unfinished Washington Monument and then turning left for a circuitous trip through the wooded marshes to the Capitol Building. "It was horrible, messy and full of stinking odors from the rancid waters, I wouldn't..."

Zack interrupted him, "Come on Putzi, this is the 1860's, buddy. People are still dumping their toilet buckets out the windows, man. What do you expect? There's more than one reason why people in the future call this place 'The Swamp!'"

Rick jumped in, as well, "The really amazing part was once we went through the shrubbery and thickets, we were standing at the base of the same exact Capitol Building that has existed all those years into the future! It was wild to see the place and yet witness a much smaller amount of people issuing forth from the exits where Hill Rats continue to use in the future. Since the outbreak of the rebellion, the sheer number of Senators and Representatives – and hence Hill Rats – had decreased significantly."

Louise and Putzi both looked at Rick, "Hill Rats?"

"Yes, yes…so sorry, the people who move from office to office as staff employees, regardless of who's been elected, reelected or 'retired' back to their home states in the last election. They never leave."

Both nodded their heads, as if understanding – though, they really didn't understand.

Zack jumped back in, "Then out of nowhere, we bumped into a gaggle of U.S. Senators and the Military Governor of Tennessee, who were all drunk, making their way back to the Capitol after a meal and libations."

Louise answered hesitantly, "So…what?"

Zack and Rick said it together, "The drunkest one in the group was Andy Johnson!"

Putzi added for clarification, "You know, the one who'll become President in the future when Lincoln will be shot. The guy's a total misfit and drunkard. We *have* to ensure Hannibal takes over as President."

Jack sardonically responded, "Thanks, Putzi, for never putting too fine a point on your pencil." Putzi didn't get it.

There was a beat of silence.

I responded, "We met Lincoln."

Rick, Zack and Putzi were dumbstruck, until Zack quickly stuttered, "Duuude, what?"

I repeated myself, "We met Abraham Lincoln."

Then, Doc and Louise took turns sharing parts of the story of our chance meeting with the 16th President of the United States.

I sat back and enjoyed the course that our conversation took next.

Zack wanted to know what Lincoln's beard looked like and how his hair was cut, "Was it more like Sting's short hair or did it have that Elvis Costello kind of puffed-up look."

Louise answered, "From the side he looked like he did on the 1909 S VDB Wheat Penny."

We all looked at her. I spoke, "The what?"

She repeated it matter-of-factly as if everyone should know, "The 1909 S VDB Wheat Penny."

Zack scrunched up his face and said "*What* are you?"

Louise responded without missing a beat, "I'm a numismatist."

Zack was speechless for a second. Then he said, "Ok… cool. I didn't know." Then Zack turned to his brother and said, "We're Baptists."

The confident footfalls of a man on a mission echoed in the lobby and interrupted our discussion. It was the Vice President of the United States. He held in his hand a piece of paper. "Folks, I found *what* we need to head back to July 4th. It's a voucher from the wagon master who took me to General Meade's Headquarters."

Doc stood up and said, "May we all go with you?"

Han Hamlin looked into each of our faces with a confidence I had not yet seen in his demeanor, and said "I wouldn't have it any other way."

Doc had us huddle together at the site of the Telluric Current One. There were eight of us: The Vice President, Louise, Doc, Jack, Putzi, Rick, Zack and me. While standing over the telluric current we each placed a finger on the signature and the DNA of the wagon master; in a split second we reversed time by a week and half and were in the *new* last day of the Battle of Gettysburg.

Section VIII

34

Gettysburg and The Last Stand

July 4th, 1863

Due to a series of sabotaged telegraph lines for three days during the Battle of Gettysburg, President Lincoln was unable to direct the course of the war via his directing the conduct of his generals. The fourth day was no different.

His custom, over the entire conduct of the war, was to direct and re-direct the troop movements of his generals by telegraph. He called the telegrams, "lightening messages." The best way I was able to more fully understand Lincoln's incredible use of technology was to compare it with my-current history's use of GPS and instant telecom opportunities, texts and electronic messages.

Yet in the single most important battle in the Civil War, Lincoln was without telegraphic "eyes or ears". The lines had been cut; he was helpless, unlike any time during his years as Commander in Chief.

On July 4th, 1863 the Vice President of the United States was actually at the battlefield in Gettysburg. Noah Brooks, the historian and eyewitness to the Battle of Gettysburg, would later write, "(Then-Vice President) Hamlin arrived to find the enemy in retreat. Mr. Hamlin was warning Commanding General Meade that he ought to follow up General Robert E. Lee, lest he should escape."

As with the previous written historical account, Brooks continued, "Meade's headquarters presented a chopfallen appearance; here I met Vice President Hamlin, who was also a visitor at Meade's headquarters, and who had been taken out to see the fight (which did not come off) at a point near Williamsport. He asked for copies of the President's telegrams and was told by Meade there were none because the President had not communicated with the General for three days. As we met, Hamlin raised his hands and turned away his face with a gesture of despair... only for a moment."

Brooks wrote, "Then he did something remarkable. Mr. Hamlin took command of the field, *as Acting President of the United States*, and therefore, *Acting Commander in Chief*, with the expressed purpose of seeing the Confederate army annihilated. General Meade refused to obey him. Hamlin relieved Meade of his command on the spot, had him arrested and appointed Gen. John Sedgewick as Commanding General. The new Acting President stood next to Gen. Sedgewick as the general rallied the Union Army to "attack and keep attacking until no rebel was left standing". Hamlin said flatly, "Today the Confederacy ends." Noah Brooks wrote down those words.

With no telegraph available, Hamlin requested that 23-year-old Brigadier General George Custer, also record in writing the events of those moments at the Field Headquarters, so that President Lincoln would have an official after-action report of what was done on the battlefield, and not just the words of a journalist. The Boy General laid down his sword on a flat surface and picked up a pencil and paper, immediately memorializing what had just happened in the Headquarters by Hamlin. Custer had a very clear and concise way of writing.

Generals Sedgewick, Butterfield and Custer all affixed their signatures as eyewitnesses to the report, relieving Meade from command. Hamlin signed it as well. Under his name he simply wrote 'Acting President of the United States, July 4th, 1863.' Custer saluted Hamlin and exited the tent, jumped on to his horse and rejoined his calvary unit.

Noah Brooks may have been a non-military eyewitness to history, but he wasn't the only one. Our band of spacetime travelers were there with John Hay at the headquarters, witnessing the courage and shear strength of character that Han Hamlin exhibited as Acting President.

We witnessed his creative understanding of American history. History books of 1863 all showed that in 1841, when then-Vice President John Tyler, was sworn in as President of the United States, upon the sudden death of incumbent President William Henry Harrison – it was the first time in American history that a sitting president passed away, thus demanding Tyler's ascension to the Presidency.

At the time, members of Harrison's Cabinet made the demand that Tyler should *only* become the "Acting President". The entire Cabinet acknowledged the concept of an 'acting president'. Tyler rejected their claims because, *of course,* his predecessor had died, leaving a void that needed to be *permanently* filled. Tyler was immediately sworn in as President, a precedent for Constitutional succession.

When John Hay and Vice President Hamlin met in the Willard Hotel to discuss what could be done, initiating the office of Acting President was a major part of their decision, the future Secretary of State later told us, "We reasoned that we had to end the war at the Battle of Gettysburg on July 4th 1863, before Lee and his troops escaped over the Potomac River."

He continued, "In 1841 during the debate on Tyer assuming the Presidency, Cabinet Secretaries Henry Clay and Daniel Webster expressed their belief in an *acting president.* Hamlin and I decided for him to exercise the rights to that long-forgotten position that was advocated by Harrison's cabinet against John Tyler. Hamlin would take charge. Knowing that doing anything other than that would prolong the war and, based on future-historical records we showed him, would cost an additional 88,000 lives – killed in battle from August 1863- April 1865, not counting those who would die from disease. We chose to make that our plan. We chose to end the war."

In preparation for this issue, Rick instructed the group, "The idea of an Acting President would be used a few times in the future 20th and 21st centuries. Each time, there were two individuals who were President of the United States *at the same time.* So, in July, 1863 Lincoln would have his authority taken over by his Vice President, at this critically important moment in history. Han Hamlin forged new ground for the first time by initiating the position of Acting President and then fully stepping into that role during battle."

The proof of the pudding, they say, is in the eating. On that 4th of July, just eighty-seven years since the signing of the Declaration of Independence, Acting President Hannibal Hamlin, General John Sedgewick, Brigadier General George Custer and other lessor known officers enacted the fourth and final day's battle plan for attacking the remaining members of Lee's army that were trapped against the Potomac River.

To quote one of the infantry officers earlier, "This was to be Bobby Lee's Last Stand." Custer nodded in agreement and said "Yes, it will be. I like the terrible sound of that expression."

And it was a terrible battle too, complete with the awful destruction of man, animal and land.

This was no Appomattox Court House surrender, no kindly armistice, no gentlemanly surrender. It was indeed a "last stand" and a slaughter. Grapeshot and bayonet charges by the Union, calvary stampedes and bloody broad sword attacks combined to shrink the body of Confederate soldiers from Army size to Corps size, to Division size; then as the blood flowed into the rising current of the Potomac River, the rebels Divisions fell in size to Brigade strength, Regiment and finally to Company and Squad size. Death was all around them. The Rebels offered no white flag. The Union Army gave no mercy.

The last 100+ soldiers of the Army of Northern Virginia soldiers were valiantly huddled together in a circle on a knoll surrounding General Robert E. Lee, all with firearms in hand, blazing away. They shouted, "No surrender, no retreat."

The Union infantry and calvary troops placed under the direction of Brigadier General George Armstrong Custer fiercely attacked the rebel remnants and annihilated them.

Lee was the last man standing. He died when Union Private John Jefferson Williams of the 34th Regiment, Indiana Infantry broke through the small dying inner circle of protective rebel officers laying on the ground around General Lee. Through his peripheral vision Williams saw a downward thrust of Lee's saber directed at him. Private Williams parried Lee's wild slash and then released a point-blank round from his .58 caliber, 40" Springfield Model 1863 rifle. At the same time, with his US M1855 Type II socket bayonet, the Union private thrust all 18 inches of it deep into the chest of General Robert E. Lee.

The former Union Colonel, former West Point Superintendent and Member of the West Point Class of 1829 and Confederate General in Chief of the entire Armies of the Confederate States of America collapsed in a bloody heap, pulling down young John Jefferson Williams as he fell to the ground. Lee's hand gripped Williams' bloody shirt and blue uniform lapel. Lee looked at his own blood on his hands, his eyes went heavenward. He seemed to search the sky. Williams later said, "Lee's last whispered words were, 'Father, into your hands I commend my spirit.'"

He was gone, along with his forces. No rebel life was left on the field, only one animal survived, Lee's horse Traveler, wounded and limping. The fourth day of Gettysburg was more brutal for the Confederates than the other three days of battle combined because it ended the war. Ironically, the final day of last battle of the two-year War Between the States was over in less than two hours. Union success by infantry and calvary through musket, cannon grapeshot, bayonet and broadsword fighting ended this un-civil war because of Han Hamlin's decision to assert himself as Commander in Chief.

The famed socket-style bayonet that pierced the heart of the Confederacy's commanding general and killed him, was removed from the body of Robert E. Lee by Dr. Troy Weeks, a Union doctor and referred to as 'The Bayonet that won the War.' The good doctor's family owned it for over 150 years.

As the silence settled in, Hamlin gathered together the troops and spoke to all in front of the Sedgewick Headquarters tent, "July 4th, 1863 will henceforth be thought of as The Day of Reckoning – a day of holding firm to our Independence. For the lashes of the slaver's whip were met today with utter destruction and death by the free man's cannon, sword and bayonet. Slavery and rebellion die this day as bloody miscarriages of freedom on this field of battle, along with the men who illegitimately fathered them." Journalist Noah Brooks took down every word. Hamlin's powerful words lasted only two and half minutes. Photographer Matthew Brady arrived earlier that day; now he captured several images of Han Hamlin addressing the soldiers. The words and images would be telegraphed across the nation. It would be called, The Gettysburg Address.

What ironically came next was a festive song. From the Union soldiers sprang the Confederacy's anthem, Dixie. At first, I expected it to be a dirge, but instead the soldiers sang it with gusto. Those Union soldiers had recently changed the words.

"Away down South in the land of traitors,
rattlesnakes and alligators,
Right away, come away, right away, come away.

Where cotton's king and men are chattels,
Union boys will win the battles,
Right away, come away, right away, come away.

Each Dixie boy must understand
That he must mind his Uncle Sam.
Away, away, away down south to Dixie."

The troops of the Union Army of the Potomac gave several cries together in one voice, "Huzzah for President Hamlin! Huzzah for Uncle John! Huzzah for the Boy General!" Repeating the expressions several times, the soldiers began to cry out with joy, and hug one another. Tears of sadness combined with shouts of sheer joy. The Civil War was over and as Doc turned and said to us, "Only we few, we happy few, we band of time-siblings helped cause its end."

Gen. Custer arrived in a cloud of dust, jumped from his horse and stood in front of the troops, "Huzzah, troops, huzzah! The telegraph line to Washington has been fixed!" He saluted Gen. John Sedgewick and Acting President Hamlin, while at the same time slapping the dust off his wide-brimmed hat and withdrawing a pencil and a small paper from his inside coat pocket.

"What do you want me to send to the President, Mr. President?" he said with a wide smirking smile. Hamlin looked at me as if to request my thoughts. I looked at our group, Doc, Louise, Putzie, Jack, Zack and Rick. Then, Zack remembered a quote from C. S. Lewis in the second book of the Space Trilogy, Perelandra; "Write this: *'All the good things are now,'*" which Custer did. Jack Lewis smiled.

Then he paused and Han Hamlin added, "Add this: 'Victory is secured. Our long national nightmare is over,'" which the Boy General added and looked around for any other possible additions. I thought about it for a second, knowing we were soon out of supplies, and turned to Rick with a historical twinkle in my eye, "Should we say, '*Come on. Be quick. Bring packs. P.S. bring pacs?*'" Rick looked up at Custer and then to me; he said as he smirked, "Nah, I think we'll be… *O.K.*"

Section IX

35

Lincoln's Response

1863 Washington D. C.

I suppose people are people, no matter what century, no matter what political situation in which they find themselves and especially no matter how horrible life becomes. But some individuals rise above the base responses to life's terrible times and show their *influence* on the world without ever having to show their *power*.

Abraham Lincoln was one of those people.

Hours after Lee's death and the annihilation of the Confederate forces on July 4th, 1863 at Gettysburg, no one in Sedgewick's HQ was quite sure what next to do, other than to wait for a response from Lincoln.

It arrived in due time: "To Acting President Hamlin (stop) Sec. Stanton said 'If the thing is pressed, I think that Lee will be finished'. Thrilled to see the thing was pressed. (stop) Next is so-called President Jeff Davis. (stop) My promise to be the only President seems short-sighted. (stop) But, as bad promises are better broken than kept, I shall now treat this as a bad promise, and break it, (stop) convinced that keeping the promise is averse to the public interest. You have led well, Mr. Acting President." (final stop)

Hamlin smiled the smile of a man who had done the right thing and had been rewarded for it. He walked over to us. "It's time for us to ride back to The Capital City and begin the hard work of effecting change to save Mr. Lincoln's life."

Louise said ruefully, "At this moment of national joy it seems heartless to begin the end of Lincoln's presidency." She paused and looked at all of us, "But it is the right thing to do."

John Hay said, "And I am the one to effect that change, whether by impeachment or not." He paused and then looked directly at Louise, "The impeachment and conviction could have more easily occurred with the Union losing the war, but the annihilation of Lee makes this less likely. I know we had to end the war to save the life of The Tycoon, that was a given – having seen history in the future. Lee's death adds another level of complexity."

Louise slowly nodded her head and added, "Or simplicity."

Hay nodded and then turned to the Acting President and continued, "Mr. Hamlin, are you willing to trust me some more?"

"Of course, I am," Hamlin said.

Hay accepted that as the open door through which he must now proceed.

"Since Impeachment and Conviction would most likely become prolonged events, dividing loyalties again after the most terrible war of our history, what if we were to appeal to the *better angels* of Mr. Lincoln's nature?"

We all looked at Hay, expecting an explanation from him.

None came. He just looked at us and stared off mystically in the distance, as he was so often prone to do.

And then, eventually, quietly, he said, "President Lincoln knows what to do. Just 11 months ago he and I worked on this precise response to an editorial response to newspaper publisher Horace Greely about saving the Union. Though I did not know it at the time, tucked within his portion of these words is the answer that Abraham Lincoln must and should now do, for himself and for the nation."

Then he looked at us and stated from memory the following:

"I would save the Union. I would save it the shortest way under the Constitution. The sooner the national authority can be restored; the nearer the Union will be the Union as it was."

If there be those who would not save the Union, unless they could at the same time save slavery, I do not agree with them.

If there be those who would not save the Union unless they could at the same time destroy slavery, I do not agree with them.

My paramount object in this struggle is to save the Union, and is not either to save or to destroy slavery.

If I could save the Union without freeing any slave I would do it, and if I could save it by freeing all the slaves I would do it; and if I could save it by freeing some and leaving others alone, I would also do that.

What I do about slavery, and the colored race, I do because I believe it helps to save the Union; and what I forbear, I forbear because I do not believe it would help to save the Union."

John Hay paused to recall the rest of the letter in his mind, then continued.

"I shall do less whenever I shall believe what I am doing hurts the cause, and I shall do more whenever I shall believe doing more will help the cause.

I shall try to correct errors when shown to be errors; and I shall adopt new views so fast as they shall appear to be true views."

John Hay looked at Hannibal Hamlin, "You are the abolitionist Mr. Lincoln never was. You are the faithful, loyal man of integrity, as opposed to myself and my deception. Yours has been a career as an influential statesman that had at its center the freedom of an entire race. Mr. Lincoln's political nature was the use of power rather than influence."

I began to see where this was going.

Hay looked at all of us, "Upon our return to Washington, we need to join you, Vice President Hamlin, as you visit with The

Tycoon. We need to invite him into the truth of what we've done and what's facing him. He will strain to understand – however, he is a man of science with a U.S. Patent himself, and by law he created the National Academy of Sciences in March of 1863 and thoroughly loves inventions and science. His dalliance with the telegraph is one such example. Even his former law partner once said Lincoln "evinced a decided bent toward machinery or mechanical appliances, a trait he doubtless inherited from his father who was himself something of a mechanic." He's a reader of history and a man who desires to return to Springfield," Hay paused. *"Alive."*

We all looked at John Hay.

Then he said, as if only to himself, "May God grant him the assurance of things not yet seen."

36

Hamlin and Lincoln

1863 Washington D. C.

Vice President Hamlin understood what his sole *and* important duty was to obtain an audience at the White House with Lincoln, for the older version of John Hay and himself. After the success at Gettysburg, this would be warmly welcomed.

John Nicolay, Lincoln's chief secretary had been sent a card by Hamlin earlier in the day requesting an audience with Lincoln. Hamlin and Hay would be available to meet with the President the next morning. Hamlin also asked that "young Hay" not be included in the meeting because it would be a "surprise" by Hay's *supposed* father. Hay would be "playing" that father, until the *veil* was removed for Lincoln. Nicolay must have been curious about the last part of that request, but he seemed to decide that father and son could be reunited after the more important meeting in the President's office. So, he scheduled the meeting in the Executive Office for The Tycoon and his guests.

Walking up to the front gate of the Executive Mansion in 1863 was surreal to me. It had always been breathtaking for me to visit the White House, even as a child. I was born in Washington

D. C. – or I should say I *will be* born there – 93 years from the current "now".

My father was in the military. He and my mother met and fell in love in the nation's capital during WWII. I was later born at Walter Reed Army Hospital. And like a permanent prop in our family's story, stood the 20th century-version of The White House, with its wrought iron anthemion-patterned fence and tightly secured front gate on Pennsylvania Avenue; inside that gated area was the well-rounded circular and beautifully paved North Drive, manicured lawn, flowers and fountain, as well as the always-guarded and locked front door to the North Portico entrance which leads directly into the Entrance Hall.

All clean, all white, all perfect. I'd visited this beautiful house as a child in the 1950's, as a ten-year-old in the 1960's, in the late 70's with my new bride, the 80's as a candidate for Congress, the 90's as a lobbyist and the 2000's as an author. I had changed, but The White House had never *really* changed. In my lifetime 14 separate Presidents had occupied this mansion – and the general theme was consistency.

Looking at The White House in 1863, however, was incredibly different.

It was less white and more smokey gray, kind of *dirty,* if you will. As we walked up the oval and less-cared-for North Drive, we passed alongside a bronze weather-beaten statue of Thomas Jefferson that had been sitting for fifteen years in the center of the oval driveway on our left as we approached the mansion, next to the unmanicured North lawn which shortly gave way to a modestly cared-for dirt walkway that paralleled the front of the White House. I looked down into an attached pit-like dingy area on the north side of the mansion, the tradesmen entrance, extending below the North Portico and into the dark basement. It seemed to only accentuate the mansion's griminess that I was viewing for the first time in my life.

As we climbed the few steps on the right side of the porch and then turned again to the right at the front door of the North Portico, I looked up and saw a sandstone 'garland and door surround' above the double door. I suppose I'd seen it before, but it caught my eye nonetheless. The sandstone etched fruit, flowers, leaves and acorns that adorned the double Scottish Roses were brilliantly white and beautiful, especially in contrast to the overall grayness I observed. I looked to the front edge of the portico and noticed there was no dismount area under the portico's roof for people arriving at the White House. Carriages off-loaded to the side and not under a covering. That lane of traffic was not *yet* under the portico. No ability for guests to exit carriages or for *future* outgoing Presidents joining *future* Presidents-elect in vehicles existed under the covering of the North Portico in 1863. Future images of cars and new Presidents on Inaugural Day, so familiar to me in history did not exist and were not even thought of for Lincoln's Executive Mansion North Portico.

Through the unguarded, paint-chipped and weather-worn wooden front doors of the White House, the Vice President of the United States Hannibal Hamlin, John Hay, our band of spacetime travelers and I walked. We were met by the echoing sound of singers – almost Christmas carolers, but it was July.

They *were* performers.

The White House Head Doorkeeper, "Old Edward" greeted the Vice President and his guests at the entrance. His Irish brogue was inviting as he opened the double doors and casually said, "We've been expecting you, Mr. Vice President." Music was playing somewhere above us.

The entrance area of the White House was a mess. So chaotic and dirty that it shook me as we entered in. Five years from now, in 1868, it would be described by future-First Lady Julia Grant as "a sober place; unbearably dark and shabby". The disarray of the entrance reception area was sickening to her. It had become a resting place for workers who heated up their lunches inside and smoked their pipes incessantly. What a terrible first impression for anyone walking in.

Old Edward then paused and nodded upwards in the direction of the singing. "The Hutchinson Family Singers" are makin' the President smile right now. Come along, I'll take you up to the second floor and let young Mr. Nicolay know that you are ready to be seen by the President. As requested, *young* Mr. Hay knows nothing of your arrival – he's actually on an errand for the President."

The *older* version of John Hay simply smiled, lost in his own memories as we entered.

We could clearly hear the lyrics of the song coming from the second floor.

HURRAH for the choice of the nation!
Our chieftain so brave and so true;
We'll go for the great Reformation—
For Lincoln and Liberty too!

They'll find what by felling and mauling
Our rail-maker statesman can do
For the people are everywhere calling
For Lincoln and liberty, too

Then up with the banner so glorious
The star-spangled red, white and blue
We'll fight 'til our banner's victorious
For Lincoln and liberty, too

We climbed the somewhat unsteady staircase to the second floor and made our way to the President's office. There in the hallway leaning against the doorpost was a laughing Abraham Lincoln, clapping in rhythm with a group of a capella singers.

As we walked down the long hallway, I turned to Zack and Rick Besso and asked them if they'd ever read about this music group. John Hay was listening to our conversation, as we walked toward the President.

Zack responded first, "*The Hutchinson Family Singers?* Are you kidding? Of course, we've read about them."

Rick added, "They're considered the *source* of protest music in America; along with spirituals sung by slaves, their protest songs were *everywhere* in the North. Sort of like Bob Dylan a hundred years from now."

John Hay asked, "Who is Bob Dylan?"

Zack responded, "He's a singer songwriter, in the future who, much like the Hutchison Family, will have an incredible impact on the nation during another time of war."

"Will he sing with his own family?" Hay asked.

Zack responded with a twinkle in his eye, "Nah, but he'll sing with the Travelling Willburys."

As we approached, someone in the a capella group *shshed* the Besso Brothers.

Both Besso Brothers ignored the sound and joined in on the remaining lyrics as we arrived at the impromptu concert in the hallway.

The singing group glanced at Zack and Rick and then returned to President Lincoln as they finished the last two verses of their ballad.

"We'll go for the son of Kentucky—
The hero of Hoosierdom through;
The pride of the Suckers so lucky—
For Lincoln and Liberty too!

Our David's good sling is unerring,
The Slaveocrats' giant he slew;
Then shout for the Freedom-preferring—
For Lincoln and Liberty too!

Lincoln clapped and thanked them as he shook their hands; it appeared the President's way of moving guests along.

Extending the palm of his right hand toward the Besso Brothers but looking at the singing family, Lincoln added, "Well it seems we have additional supporters of your fine protest folk music!"

Jesse Hutchinson, Jr. smiled the smile of a somewhat upstaged entertainer and quietly said, "So it seems, Mr. President."

Lincoln thanked the Hutchinson Family Singers, one by one, shaking their hands and handing them off to Old Edward for him to take the group downstairs and to the exit.

The Vice President spoke first, "Mr. President, for our meeting today I don't want to overwhelm you with such a large group, so I'd like to have *Father* Hay, Dr. Gersema and myself solely in the meeting with you. Our other friends have agreed to wait out in the hallway until we are done."

Lincoln looked somewhat cockeyed at Hamlin and said with a chuckle. "Well, Han, what additional entertainment do you have up your sleeve? How about if we also ask these two impromptu singers to join us?"

Zack and Rick looked at each other, not expecting an invitation to be extended by Lincoln. Hamlin nodded to them; both brothers offered their awkward acceptance at the same time and moved forward with the smaller group. "Alright Mr. President," Hamlin said.

Lincoln added "Whatever the nature of this meeting is, we need to celebrate with some music and mirth, *especially* after the hero you have become, Han."

As they closed the door, I glanced at Louise, Jack and Putzi and then looked down the hallway as I heard footfalls coming our way. Young John Hay advanced towards us with a number of files in his hands and a look of question in his eyes.

"May I help you?" he asked.

Section X

37

"This is the end, my only friend." - The Doors

1863 Near Irwinville, Georgia

History books would soon tell us how the 1863 version of the Confederacy collapsed even quicker than did its 1865 counterpart. The tide rolled hard with Lee's death in battle. It caused a deep panic throughout the Southern states. President Jefferson Davis alone survived to lead them, but in name only. Their economy imploded with the impact of the Emancipation Proclamation, originally proclaimed on January 1st 1863, but truly taking effect just days ago on July 4th with the annihilation of the Confederate Army of Northern Virginia. The labor shortage, due to newly freed slaves escaping to the North, halted cotton production, as fall harvest loomed ahead. There were simply no laborers to pick it. With the withdrawal from the CSA of even the most minimal diplomatic support from the British Empire and France, there remained not even the *possibility* of allies to help. Jefferson

Davis wrote a friend at this time, "(T)here's a depression which is spreading like a starless night over the country. The war had now shrunk into narrow proportions."

In fact, Davis himself chose to escape Richmond, in hopes of securing entry to Mexico or joining with the few remaining ragtag groups of rebels in Texas. He would make it only halfway across Georgia.

Jefferson Davis was found at a campsite in a twelve-acre field near Irwinville, Georgia with his family. A newly-freed slave, 53-year-old Willis Williams formerly of faraway Greene County, recognized Davis and led Union Troopers, from a Michigan unit, to his camp. Williams would gain fame both as the man who helped find fugitive Jefferson Davis but also as the Great-grandfather of future President M.L. King, Jr. In 1863 Williams became a national hero.

Jefferson Davis' small band of supporters fought an unsuccessful skirmish. During this brief defense, Davis mounted his horse to escape and in a matter of a mere fifteen yards was met by a Union calvary trooper and ordered to halt and surrender. Davis jumped from his horse, dropped a shawl and a raglan from his shoulders and advanced aggressively toward the trooper who had leveled his carbine directly at the President of the Confederate States of America. The trooper again commanded that Davis halt and surrender. In a moment of added confusion, Davis' wife threw herself in front of her husband, surprising the Union Trooper who accidently squeezed off one solitary .44 caliber round from his Remington M1858 New Army weapon. That single round instantly killed both husband and wife... as well as the rest of the Confederate States of America.

The hopes of the South lay crumpled at the Union trooper's feet, with two lovers lying dead on the trampled grass of a temporary military campsite in rural Georgia.

The capture of remaining Confederate guerillas throughout the South took place in the late summer and early fall of 1863. It proved equally successful and equally brutal.

But before all that would happen, the Vice President's meeting with the man, Abraham Lincoln, had to occur – and occur it did.

The Executive's office door closed as the President, the Vice President, *older* John Hay, Dr. Russ Gersema and the Besso Brothers moved into the Executive Office.

The rest of us turned as a group to meet *younger* John Hay, striding towards us with files in hands, motioning us into his office. He and William Stoddard had desks and multiple chairs crammed together in a limited space, as these two of three private secretaires served the President. Only one had a nameplate on his desk. It read: William Osborn Stoddard, Private Secretary to the President.

We found in our short visit that Nicolay and *young* Hay experienced Stoddard to be irritating and self-promoting. "Stod" and Hay were on permanent "loan" to The White House from two other Federal Departments. John G. Nicolay, the only official Private Secretary, was chosen specifically by the President. His personal office was next to President Lincoln's office, within which the current meeting with Vice President Hamlin and our friends was taking place. This office was spacious compared to that of the other two secretaries, in which we now found ourselves.

Stoddard and *young* Hay's office was directly across the hallway from The Tycoon. Jack Lewis, using a clever turn of a phrase that he would one day return to when writing The Voyage of the Dawn Treader, noticed the antipathy between "Stod" and the others and mentioned in a low tone, "There was a boy called William Osborn Stod, and he almost deserved it."

Young Hay laughed as he overheard it.

As Hay invited us into the cramped office, he introduced himself and, signaled to an obviously irritated Stoddard to surrender his chair for the lady in our group. Stoddard complied and Louise took the offer of his chair. We began to talk.

"What may I do for you fine people?" began the 25-year-old version of our *older* friend who was at this very minute across the hallway. Hay's speech pattern was a strong clipped business-like fashion, that can only harden anyone in such an exalted position, at such a young age, as a result of the blast furnace of war. He was all business.

Louise took the lead, "Our friends are with the Vice President, visiting your friend, The Tycoon…" She stopped, realizing how informal she was and how intimate the expression was that she just used.

Hay was surprised and taken aback somewhat.

"Oh, please forgive me, I should have said 'The President'"

Hay interrupted her, "How do you know of that title – *The Tycoon*? No one outside of Mr. Nicolay and myself use that particular expression. How did you come by it?"

I saw that Louise was searching for a proper spacetime response and I began to rapidly think of the options, when Putzi interjected in German.

"Mein Herr, all the leaders in Bavaria are called 'Tycoon'".

Surprised, Hay responded in German, "My German is good, but did I understand you correctly? All the leaders of Bavaria?" He paused, collecting his thoughts, as he moved from German to English, and continued, "I understood it to only be a Japanese word."

I saw that Putzi was covering up for Louise's gaffe by creating a pattern interrupt in a different language. Of course, it was a lie, but it helped us avoid any further pokes or prods from young Hay, as they switched back to English, so that, according to Hay, "the young lady would not feel awkward", believing that German was unknown to her. Louise laughed at young Hay's arrogance and dismissive response about her supposed lack of language ability. After years of living abroad in Austria, Louise understood every word. She nodded to Putzi when he winked at her and said "So sorry Miss Louise, we were just discussing comedy and young Mr. Hay says he was simply trying to tease you about using the name, 'Tycoon.'"

Although we were in a lying contest in one office, young Hay had no idea about the truth that was being delivered next door to Mr. Lincoln in another office.

Louise responded directly to Hay, "Thank you for your sense of humor, sir. You are indeed a gentleman. And so young a gentleman at that!"

Hay seemed to blush a bit.

She continued, "While our friends discuss matters of interest with President Lincoln, would you mind telling us what you hope to do with your own future once the Union is victorious in this War of Rebellion?"

Hay smiled at Louise, Jack, Putzi and me – a sort of boyish smile – and then responded, "Well, since… *The Tycoon*… is scheduled for a long discussion with the Vice President and your friends… you seem to need nothing from me except my future life's story." He laughed. "So, I will bend your ear a bit," he put down his armful of files on an already cluttered desk, stood leaning against the corner of the desk. He looked at the other private secretary and said to William Stoddard, who was still hanging about, "Stod, please head down to the White House baker and fetch us some of the President's corn cakes for us to enjoy, won't you?"

"*Fetch* us?" Stoddard asked incredulously, as if feeling like he was someone's butler, *or dog.*

Hay diplomatically responded to us, "Mr. Stoddard is the favorite among the private secretaries to President Lincoln's family. He's the only one who can 'get his way' on domestic issues in this White House with The First Lady."

Then moving his right index finger up and down toward Stoddard, Hay said "Mrs. Lincoln loves the way Stod gets things done. He's more well thought of than Nico and me by Mrs. Lincoln."

Stoddard suddenly changed and took on the slight appearance of a pufferfish, "Well, I do have a certain way with the Lincoln family and their servants listen to me. I don't like to say too much, but Mr. Hay is accurate… How many of Mr. Lincoln's corn cakes should I get?"

"Let's get enough for all of us – and some for the Tycoon's guests. Oh, and remember to get two for Mr. Lincoln, himself." Hay turned and waited for Stoddard to jump in with Stoddard's oft repeated (and therefore expected) comment.

"Stod" didn't disappoint.

"The President says that he can eat as many corn cakes in a single sitting as two women could cook, one after another."

Stoddard turned and exited; a departed, happy, self-congratulated 'intimate' friend of Abraham Lincoln.

We all paused as the sound of his footfalls deceased in volume the further down the hallway he proceeded, until they turned a corner and lessened.

Hay looked at us, "Well, that should keep him occupied for at least the time we need!'

We couldn't contain ourselves; we all laughed out loud.

38

John Hay's Future

1863 Washington D. C.

Louise continued her questions to *young* John Hay, "So… what *do* you hope to do with your life, after the White House?"

Hay looked at the threadbare carpet in his shabby office. "I want to follow Mr. Lincoln home to Springfield, when this is all over. I'd be honored to practice law with him." He paused, then continued, "He's a good businessman and was relatively wealthy before this Presidency descended on his shoulders. People call him 'Old Abe' but he only just turned 54 a few months ago. John Adams lived to almost 91, Jefferson to 83, Madison to 85 and even that Rebel turncoat, former President John Tyler, died last year at almost 72 years of age. I think The Tycoon can have a long and wonderful life. As well, Nico and I plan to help him write his memoirs."

Putzi innocently asked, "Will Herr Stoddard help, too?"

Hay held eye contact with Putzi for the longest time, then answered. "No, he'll be too busy running for some office somewhere, letting people know how valuable he was to President Lincoln …"

And then young John Hay broke into a most mischievous smile. "And losing..."

I looked up at the ceiling to avoid publicly relishing this little bit of historical *cattiness* and *utter dismissal.*

Hay continued, "And... I hope I'll find a lovely young Illinois lady, settle down in Springfield and have many children."

Louise smiled and nodded.

I next asked him about his friendship with the Lincoln boys.

"Bob Lincoln's certainly *afternoonified* and he's *benjo* and *bricky,* all at the same time."

We all sort of looked at one another.

I wanted to ask if he was *jiggy* with all that, but decided not to. Again, the American version of the English language has its very odd moments – century after century.

"Hmm, sounds like a decent guy," I responded, hoping the pleasant tone of Hay's voice (rather than these strange words) illustrated that Bob Lincoln was a pal of *young* John Hay.

He was.

Hay continued, "Oh, don't you kid yourself, Bob is a Todd much more than he is a Lincoln. He can be every bit as prickly as his mother, Mary *Todd* Lincoln; yet he's still a driven young man – much as I've been charged as being. We enjoy a good whiskey together."

I continued, "What about Tad?"

"Tad's got a remarkable sense of honor. He's always dressing up as a soldier and marching alongside the Union troops that guard the Executive Mansion. His speech impediment is quite noticeable when you first meet him, but for me, over these few years, it just melts away – he's such a loving young man – a lot like his brother, Willie was."

And then with a tone of sadness in her voice, Louise asked, "What about Willie? What was he like before he passed away last year here in the White House?"

Hay smiled sadly and said, "Willie was a hay-bale of fun. He had his father's *large* sense of humor. He loved people and was loved by the White House staff and others. Cabinet Members and many national leaders enjoyed shaking the hand of this little man, whenever they met him in the White House and *then* carried on conversations with him. He was *that* unusual for a ten-year-old boy. We all saw him as the favorite of his parents. Maybe our favorite, too."

He continued, "The Tycoon played with his younger sons as though he was their age – a lot of horseplay and hi-jinks."

He paused, emotionally moved by the memories and then quietly added. "He died a year ago, when he and his little brother came down with the typhoid. Tad survived."

Hay looked up at a ceiling corner in his office and recalled from memory a portion from an article, "'With all the splendor that was around this little fellow in his new home he was so bravely and beautifully himself – and that only. A wildflower transplanted from the prairie to the hothouse, he retained his prairie habits, unalterably pure and simple, till he died.' Willie's friend and noted poet Nathaniel Parker Willis wrote those words about the little man, who was beloved by all."

We remained quiet.

Hay interrupted himself *and* the silence, "I'm so sorry for the emotion that's surrounding this discussion, but we've all learned through this terrible war the reality of death as a part of life, haven't we? In fact, Miss Louise would you mind reaching over to that file in the far corner, entitled Letters of Support and holding on to it for a second?"

"Sure," Louise said and she took it from the table. It was a rather thin file.

Hay continued, "President Lincoln never had a single public or private communication with former President Franklin Pierce. That is, until Willie died. In fact, in the press, Pierce was a Northerner who supported slavery had been repeatedly critical of The Tycoon. Jealous that Lincoln was *successfully* in charge rather than he? *Maybe,* I'm not sure. But what I am sure of is that we received this letter from former President Pierce shortly after Willie's funeral."

Hay's skill at educating people was evident, even as a 25-year-old young man he was a teacher. "Before you hear the contents of the letter, know this; on January 6, 1853, a train carrying newly-minted President-elect Pierce, his wife, and their only son, Bennie, left Andover, Massachusetts. Not too long after departing the depot, the passenger car within which they were seated detached from the train over hilly terrain and there was a horrible accident. None of the adult passengers were seriously injured… just one small boy: 11-year-old Benjamin Pierce. He was thrown from the detached train car and his head was gruesomely crushed, nearly severed from his neck – right in front of his terribly traumatized parents. This all happened just before Pierce became President."

We reacted in absolute revulsion.

Pointing to Louise, who was clutching the file folder, Hay asked quietly, "Would you mind reading it?"

Louise tried to recover her composure. She opened the file folder and withdrew a handwritten letter, folded in a way to make its own envelope, from that single sheet of paper.

> "*Concord N. H.*
> *March 4 1862*
>
> *My dear Sir,*
>
> *The impulse to write you, the moment I heard of your great domestic affliction was very strong, but it brought back the crushing sorrow which befell me just before I went to Washington in 1853, with such power that I felt your grief, to be too sacred for intrusion.*

Even in this hour, so full of danger to our Country, and of trial and anxiety to all good men, your thoughts, will be, of your cherished boy, who will nestle at your heart, until you meet him in that new life, when tears and toils and conflict will be unknown.

I realize fully how vain it would be, to suggest sources of consolation.

There can be but one refuge in such an hour, — but one remedy for smitten hearts, which, is to trust in Him "who doeth all things well", and leave the rest to —

"Time, comforter & only healer
When the heart hath broke"

With Mrs. Pierce's and my own best wishes — and truest sympathy for Mrs. Lincoln and yourself

I am, very truly,
Yr. friend
Franklin Pierce

Louise stopped and re-read one line "…*w*hen tears and toils and conflict will be unknown."

Not one of us could speak.

39

The Decision is Made

1863 Washington D. C.

After 4 hours, the meeting in the President's Executive Office came to an apparent conclusion. At last, the door was opened and attendees began to exit. Lincoln and Hamlin stood talking together in a neighborly manner, with arms crossed, as neighbors often do, having just jointly witnessed or overcome a very difficult common experience.

The Colonel, Doc, Rick and Zack exited with a clear hint of intensity *and* resolve on their faces. Our four spacetime friends looked as people do when they've experienced something that's both traumatic and life-giving at the same time. Yet, this type of look seemed multiplied many times over in the four of them.

As Colonel Hay exited, he immediately entered *young* Hay's office, prompted, it seemed, by a sort of 'muscle memory'. He just simply walked in, as he'd done a thousand times in his youth. Even he looked surprised by his own action. On this occasion, as a man in his 60's, he'd obviously not planned (nor expected) to come face to face with the younger version of himself, seated on top of the desk, legs crossed at the ankles in a comfortable sort of fashion that young men so often do. Nor had I anticipated that I would be in the audience. Yet here I was.

Young John Hay turned to Colonel Hay and bluntly said, "My heavens, you could pass as my father." He paused, "Are we related?"

The Colonel stopped his stride, paused a moment, gathered his thoughts and then answered, "You tell me", as he extended his right hand, as a pattern interrupt to change the momentum of the discussion, a trick of the diplomatic trade he had long ago – or in this case – long into the future learned by serving two additional Presidents, beyond Lincoln. "You tell me…"

By professional instinct, young Hay uncrossed his legs and immediately slid off of his desk, "My sincerest apologies, sir, for such informality." As he grasped Hay's outstretched palm, issuing a polite 19th century soft handshake. "I am John Hay, Private Secretary to the President. And you are?"

The Colonel responded, "Mr. Bob Dylan"

Our group was caught off guard and didn't quite know how to respond to The Colonel's quick wit. Having experienced something akin to this in our previous adventure, Doc and I picked up on as we did when we met the Beatles as Willie Nelson and Peter Frampton. (That's for another time to tell…) I was first. "Yes, Mr. Dylan is from Springfield and has known the President for quite some time."

Young Hay responded, "That's odd, I've never heard his name mentioned by the Tyc… by the President." Turning to his older self, as if desiring to place his face and name, the young version asked him, "Where, in relation to the President's home, do you reside in Springfield?'

The older responded without hesitation, "9th and Jackson, one street over from his and Mary's home. I remember when they bought it in 1844. It was much smaller – only a single floor – they bought it from Rev. Dresser, who just two years before had officiated their wedding service. As I remember it, the President bought it for $1,200 cash and he also traded a lot worth $300.

It was a pretty little thing, a single-story home, painted white, it had green shutters. It was, as Mary's niece put it, 'sweet and fresh and Mary loved it.'"

The younger Hay responded, "Well, Mr. Dylan, you know that house well!"

"I should! I remember when they added the top floor – I think it was just a year after you went off to college at Brown University."

Young Hay, a bit off guard, responded, "Yes, in 1856. I was, umm, gone, until 1860 when I returned to Springfield to study law under my Uncle Milton, who introduced me to Mr. Lincoln, who offered a job to work aside Mr. Nicolay."

The Colonel was having too much fun with this. "You and that Bavarian Nico, along with Bob Lincoln used to love your whiskey there, during the campaign?'

"Umm, well, not really..."

"I think Bob Lincoln would say differently!" *Bob Dylan* said with a chuckle. Then he glanced at Zack and finished with "No need to *protest*... I'd enlist Bob Lincoln and we 'Bobs' would find a way to win the debate against you!" The Colonel was now laughing.

The *younger* took full inventory of the *older* and in a wondering and queer way, said "I have to be getting on with office work. I am a very busy man, working for the President. So sorry to rush you along. It's been very nice to meet you, Mr. Dylan," as he motioned to his office door for us to leave.

The Colonel paused the rhythm of our departure and asked his younger self, more as a statement than as a question, "You like poetry, don't you?"

"Why, yes I do," young Hay responded awkwardly.

"Here are some quick verses for you to enjoy; possibly even as a way to encourage yourself as you age."

"Please, by all means..." the young man (and future published poet) responded, leaning back against his desk.

Colonel Hay cleared his throat and then preceded his delivery with this, "It's a portion of the poem *The Enchanted Shirt,* near the end. I know the author."

At last, as they came to a village gate,
A beggar lay whistling there;
He whistled and sang and laughed and rolled
On the grass in the soft June air.

The weary (King's) couriers paused and looked
At the scamp so blithe and gay;
And one of them said, "Heaven save you, friend!
You seem to be happy to-day."

"Oh, yes, fair sirs," the rascal laughed,
And his voice rang free and glad,
"An idle man has so much to do
That he never has time to be sad."

"This is our man," the courier said;
"Our luck has led us aright.
I will give you a hundred ducats, friend,
For the loan of your shirt to-night."

The merry blackguard lay back on the grass,
And laughed till his face was black;
"I would do it, God wot," and he roared with the fun,
"But I haven't a shirt to my back."

Young Hay smiled slightly, wondering (it seemed) why such poetry was extended to him. He thanked his older self for the time *and* the poem, then shook hands – with the older version holding on just a second or so longer than is customary – and then, leaning into young Hay's right ear, he whispered, "Listen and learn, Johnny, Listen and learn."

Young Hay seemed a bit taken aback by the older man's informality with him.

Awkwardly, young '*Johnny*' responded with a comment, quite inane, "Will we be meeting one another in Springfield when this Presidency is completed?"

The Colonel thoughtfully responded, "Yes, I'd bet we'll be meeting one another on a regular basis once Mr. Lincoln returns home to Springfield." He paused, "I'll give you the shirt off my back, if you need collateral for that bet."

Young John Hay nodded respectfully and said, "Something tells me you really would do that…"

"I wouldn't have done so when I was young, but The Tycoon changed me as I grew older." Then he ended with, "Listen and learn, *Mr. Hay,* listen and learn."

With that, we started our exit from The White House, now in the able hands of two men of courage, President Lincoln and former-Acting President Hamlin.

Section XI

40

Why are we each here?

1863 Washington D. C.

History is fluid.

Most people don't agree with that statement. They seem to experience the path of history as being singular in nature, chronological, firm and knowable. What we read in history books *does* capture the bullet points of what happened – often in an accurate but limited way. What it can't tell us is what *didn't* happen.

History emanates from a fixed point in time and travels through a series of choices by mankind. Those choices produce results and effects that alter each person's life – ultimately bringing them to the day of his or her death. It sounds logical and sequential. Because we see it, we trust in it. We know it to be true.

Yet, it gets a little weird at points. Isaac Newton's three laws of science explain the weirdness: (1) Every object moves in a straight line unless acted upon by a force.

(2) The acceleration of an object is directly proportional to the net force exerted and inversely proportional to the object's mass. (3) For every action, there is an equal and opposite reaction.

I've paid particularly close attention to how these clear and accurate laws apply to a person's life – from cradle to grave. They're applicable, as well, to clans, tribes, nation-states, leagues and the global community. They begin, (and tend to go in a straight line towards something), they flourish (yet are impacted by something else), then they decline (at varying speeds of acceleration) and then they end (because other forces have acted upon them) … bringing forth a new sprout, a new blade of grass from where they crashed and decayed.

Each nation, every reich, kingdom-after-kingdom will fall. All become empires of dirt – eventually becoming decayed, unharvested crops, turned-over by the spade held in the hands of others, covered up by the blowing soil. Each land's history eventually forgotten or, worse yet, partially-reconstructed by liars. No one from those epochs ever remains alive to confirm the truth of their days. Mankind therefore wonders out loud – every generation, each empire asks the same question: "Why were we here?"

How do we know that to be absolutely true? Because all individuals ask that same question of themselves near the end of their lives – *Why am I here?* Ultimately, it's a simple proof, as people live and die, so do nations. No matter what the century – every country becomes an empire of dirt. Only souls survive; and that's why Christ's Kingdom is not of this world.

As our tribe of spacetime travelers exited young John Hay's White House office we walked past the closed door of the President's office and down the hallway to the dilapidated stairs. Old Edward said farewell to us, as he probably had a thousand other anonymous guests as he ushered us out of the Pennsylvania Avenue door onto the North Portico. With his polished demeanor and his Irish charm on full display, he opened the door and said "Now, don't you be letting this be an Irish leave!"

We looked at one another curiously. Jack Lewis simply said to Old Edward. "Goodbye…for now." And just like that, we walked out the door.

We exited the White House, returning to the Willard Hotel having decided, as we walked along Pennsylvania Avenue, to stay one additional day. We wanted to see the results of our actions. We wanted to see Newton's laws work in front of our very eyes.

'Why am I here?' asks mankind, one person at a time.

We found out that Abraham Lincoln knew the answer to *his* question.

41

Successfully Completed the Task

1863 Washington D. C.

Waking up in Washington D. C. on a July morning, *in any century*, can have either one of two climate aspects meet a traveler. One aspect, could be the relatively cool and calming of an early morning, with breezes off the Potomac River. Or, the other aspect could be the terribly uncomfortable heat and humidity that makes people wish they were either not in D. C. or not alive. We awoke on a cool morning and walked back to the White House.

Han Hamlin had requested our presence.

Contrary to what politicians and cartoonists would later write, the city was never built upon a swamp. It's truly hot, it's definitely humid but 'a steam bath does not make a swamp', as a historian would pen in the Smithsonian Magazine in the future. During the worst of the July heat, Abraham Lincoln was fond of seasonally residing with his family in the cottage at the Soldier's Home, just three miles away. The Lincolns moved all their personal possessions, including beds, to the Home from June through November of each year.

Though, on the evening of July 7th, the President found empty guest beds and spent the night at The White House. His family was with him. Young John Hay was directed to have photographer Matthew Brady set up his camera and to be ready to photograph the next morning's events.

On the morning of July 8th, 1863, in the continuing cool shade of the White House's North Portico, President Abraham Lincoln stood wearing his recognizable stovepipe hat, Vice President Hannibal Hamlin by his side bareheaded, along with Secretary of State Seward and General Fessenden of Maine; all stood elevated on the North Portico in front of newspaper journalists and a small assorted audience, including the families of Mr. Lincoln and Mr. Hamlin, below them at the carriage driveway level. Placing his spectacles on, Mr. Lincoln read the following:

"Good morning,

Throughout this recent Rebellion I have been entirely focused on saving the Union. It has been my sole goal, my reason for existence and my guiding light in the very dark days of civil discord and insurgency.

Those days are now behind us.

This week, on July 4th, 1863 the rebellion was ended and the Union was reunited, as a direct result of the leadership of Vice President/Acting President Hannibal Hamlin."

Lincoln nodded to Hamlin. The assembled journalists and assorted audience members, including their two families and those of us from spacetime travel, gave a robust ovation, causing Lincoln to pause for a moment.

Lincoln smiled and collected himself. Matthew Brady captured that image and then began reloading for a second photograph.

"I am here today to announce to the nation that I have successfully completed those duties and that my term of responsibilities is now over.

Therefore, I shall resign the Presidency in your presence, today. Vice President Hamlin will then be sworn in as President. No longer Acting President, he shall assume complete control over the entire Executive Branch of the Government."

The crowd gasped and people physically reacted, some taking a knee. Others fanning themselves aggressively, some immediately mopping their brows. Brady's second photograph was unstable, wobbly, motion-sensitive and out of focus. It seemed to capture the emotions of the crowd – confused and dazed. He moved to reload for his third and final photograph. He seemed frantic in his actions.

My fellow spacetime travelers and I took in every moment of this event. Zack, Rick and Jack appeared as interested in Matthew Brady's responses and actions as of any other journalist in attendance. Louise, Putzi and I stayed focused on watching Lincoln and Hamlin.

The President held up his hand to quiet the journalists and the small audience and continued, "In all the decisions I have made in my Presidency, I have always tried to do what was best for the Union. Throughout the long and difficult period of this Rebellion, I have felt it was my duty to preserve the Union – whether slavery ended or whether it did not end. I *am* thankful that God saw fit to use me as an instrument of ending it. On that point alone, I am a man most changed.

"I made every possible effort to complete the tasks set before me during my term of office, 'not knowing when or whether ever' I would be returning with my family to Springfield; where my children were all born and two are now buried.

As I said to my friends in Springfield when I set out for Washington, I repeat to the nation today, 'Trusting in Him who can go with me, and remain with you, and be everywhere for good, let us confidently hope that all will yet continue to be well'.

"So…also as St. Paul wrote, 'I have fought a good fight, I have finished *my* course, I have kept the faith.' To His care commending you, as I hope in your prayers you will commend President Hamlin and me, I bid you an affectionate farewell."

He handed his letter of resignation to Secretary of State Seward and invited General Fessenden to administer the Oath of Office to the Vice President.

Samuel Fessenden, a noted attorney and militia general, was Hamlin's mentor both in law and in becoming an avid abolitionist. He was Lincoln's personal choice as an alternative to pro-slavery Chief Justice Roger Taney, who had purposely not been invited by the President to be present at this national transfer of power. His snub of Taney planted the final smirk on Lincoln's face.

As the brief ceremony concluded, citizen Abraham Lincoln saluted President Hamlin, left the North Portico, waved to his three private secretaries, Hay, Nicolay and Stoddard and then looked towards Pennsylvania Avenue and paused for just a few seconds… and smiled. A flash went off and a very happy Matthew Brady stepped out from behind the camera.

Citizen Abraham Lincoln along with his family boarded the carriage, pulled by Old Bob and three other horses; Abraham Lincoln took the reins and drove it in the direction of the Soldiers Home and together they rode the first leg of Abraham Lincoln's return to Springfield.

He waved to only one other man. As Walt Whitman later wrote, "I saw the president almost every day, as I happened to live where he passed to or from his lodgings out of town. I can still see very plainly Abraham Lincoln's dark brown face, with the deep-cut lines, the eyes, always to me with a deep latent sadness in the expression. Only on that day he wore a smile as bright as the sun. He and I float in the same stream. We are grounded in the same soil. He had once been a man acquainted with many sorrows. But no longer. I returned his wave."

Whitman spoke for every citizen of the world in 1863 and since. Our work, too, in 1863 was successfully completed. So, we began saving others…

Section XII

42

One Hundred Years Later

1963 Dallas, Texas

A century passes so very slowly. 100 years, 1200 months, 36,500 days.

But not for us.

The trip from 1863 to 1963 blurred by in nanoseconds. We were all extremely joyous amending spacetime and moving on to see how that had impacted the history we had once known.

'Landing' in Dallas on November 18th 1963, just four days before what we hoped would be the unsuccessful attempted-assassination of President John F. Kennedy, would allow us to review what had indeed happened in history during the last 887,000 hours since being with *A. Lincoln.*

The document Doc used to guide us to Dallas on the 18th was a Dallas Police Department memo he possessed, having signatures of Dallas Chief of Police Jesse E. Curry, Assistant Chief Charles Batchelor, and Deputy Chief N. T. Fisher when they met and signed off on the details of the motorcade and possible routes.

His collection of autographs, books and memos was remarkable.

We held this different, more modern document on July 8th, 1863 and touched their signatures as we stepped onto Telluric Current 1 and immediately arrived at the Dallas Municipal Building on Harwood Street on November 18th 1963. Doc had done his homework. The relatively new Dallas Central Library was only a one-minute walk from that building.

Built in 1954 on the site of an original 1901 Carnegie Library building, the Dallas Central Library housed immense resources for us to review and evaluate the movement of history and the lives of those who guided it. All of us were ready to see new history through our spacetime involvement. Though our main purpose was to save President Kennedy's life, we also wanted to know what had *truly* changed in America and in the world, post the Lincoln Presidency.

The early morning of November 18th in Dallas was exactly what it would be on November 22nd – light rain and showers of rain. Sunshine would only occasionally pierce through the clouds.

My emotions during the brief walk to the library reminded me of how I felt as a kid on Christmas morning – excited, inquisitive and a bit worried. My worries on the many December 25th's of my youth were connected to concern that any unmet expectations of gifts *not* received, would dampen the gifts that *were* received. I felt the same way as our group entered the massive modern library building built by noted architect George Dahl. Doc's 'Christmas list' had each of our names on it along with corresponding areas we would naturally investigate.

"Howdy, y'all, may I help ya?" asked a perky, blonde librarian in her mid-twenties, at the main counter. Her name badge said 'Midge Galloway.'

Zack couldn't resist, "Yes ma'am, I'm lookin' to get hitched and I'm hopin' you have a twin sister, cause Lord almighty, you've gotta be married with how pretty *you* look!"

Midge blushed and shook her head, saying "No, sir. I'm not married and I do not have a sister but I DO believe that it's possible to fall in love at first sight... for *boys*, that is." She then laughed.

We all paused, then she let the other shoe drop. "You ain't by chance travelin' with a single brother who believes in haircuts, are ya?" All eyes moved toward Rick (and his high-and-tight haircut).

Midge turned to Rick.

Rick laughed and responded, "Why yes, Midge, I *am* his brother, but I *can*..." he paused and took on a Texan accent, "...*I can guaren-stinkin-tee* you that neither of us has the...um *time, right now,* to bother you with anything more than a request for a study room here at the library for our whole group to meet in for the next few days and maybe a recommendation of a place to stay. Is that possible?"

Midge shot him a mock look of hurt, being playfully downhearted for a second, "Well, yes...So, that means you'll still be around here for a few days?"

Zack nodded bashfully, as someone who asked for a date but was clearly turned down. "Until the 22nd of November," he said.

"The President will be in a parade on the 22nd; at least I think it's that day," she said.

"Are you going to see him?" Zack asked.

"You mean in person, on the street? I hadn't thought about it. I was just going to look out the library's windows..."

Zack responded, "I think it might be worth your while to go down to the street and watch. You might see me there!"

"Well, I just *might-should,"* Midge answered.

The Besso Brothers and I looked at one another with a perplexed response to her odd Texan phrase.

Doc interrupted, "Which study room would allow us the greatest chance to be focused *and* for which we would not have others submit requests?"

Pointing at a layout of the library, Midge said, "I think this one *might oughta* work."

Zack responded, "Well, maybe we might would could, together."

Midge chuckled and turned towards Doc, who obviously was in charge.

Doc signed the reservation sheet allowing us the use of the room for several days and Midge showed us the way. "Oh, and I'll check on some hotel rooms downtown for ya'll," Midge added.

As we entered the room and shut the door, I asked Zack, "What was that all about with the young lady?" I suppose my voice was harsher than I had expected it to be. Zack shrugged. It was awkward, but I was ok in letting it be, considering I had just observed a new experience of inter spacetime flirting…

Doc and Rick took over once we entered the conference room. Rick said, "Well folks, we're going to be here every day until closing; and up to noon on the 22nd. Our goal is two-fold: first we need to work out the specific step-by-step plan to save JFK's life – and that'll take some time to get organized. Second, let's dig into how history was changed since we left 1863, in case there's something we'll really need to know as we move forward with the plan. We now have four days. Let's get moving."

43

Preparing to Save Kennedy

1963 Dallas

It wasn't so much that we were assigned by Rick and Doc certain things in history to read at the Central Dallas Library in November, 1963; Doc's way is too organic for that.

Instead, we each gravitated to areas about which we held personal interests, just as we had when we earlier first examined the possible world without Hitler.

Louise and Doc wanted to know about their Jewish families – and the net effect of the American Civil War (and Lincoln's resignation actions) on the crown heads of Europe and their treatment of the Jews. Putzi did, as well. His focus was on Austria and Germany; looking at the rise and fall of Ernst Rohm instead of Hitler. In particular, Putzi wanted to know if Rohm's militarism was successfully deflected by the United States in either one or two world wars.

I wanted to know about the ripple effect of Hamlin's ascendancy to the Presidency on future generations and future presidents and generals. I also wanted to know about John Hay's future.

So did John Hay. His attention was deep in the trove of American history books about the post-Lincoln presidency.

Jack Lewis wandered over to the literature rows and spent time in deep dives about Tolkien and the other Inklings. He also spent time reading about the Civil Rights movement in America, especially about Robert Kennedy and M.L. King and where they were headed in 1963 and beyond.

Zack Besso immersed himself in something new to people in 1963, something called "the pop culture" section – finding out everything he could regarding rock'n'roll music, including those who performed it and those who produced it.

Rick Besso was most curious about Indochina, Viet Nam and the military actions that proceeded (or didn't) from the Eisenhower Administration on. He wasn't even sure there was an Eisenhower Administration…

Though the agendas were individually organic, there were certain common daily things that were stationary. Like lunch.

As Midge brought small snacks into our newly converted research room of the library, she mentioned that she had dear friends, the Cuellars, who owned a small Mexican food café in the downtown section of Dallas called *El Chico.* She told us how they had "unusual food" called "tay-cos" and "encheeladas" that tasted terrific – and that she would be honored to see if they would package up dishes for her to bring to us.

"Oh, *Cool... Take-out food!* Zack said.

"No… it's *hot* food, not cool or even cold food," she rationally responded, then added, "… and we don't *take it out* to them, they cook it up *and I go bring it back…* to us."

Midge looked at Zack with a wince, then laughingly said, "You *Yankees* speak kinda funny."

"I'm a Mariner's fan…." Zack said as an immediate reaction. "I hate the Yankees"

Midge cocked her head and then slowly said, "Well there may be hope for you, after all. I can tell you this – the South lost and whether you and I like it, we better get over it, boy. The times, they are a'changin."

John Hay pointed his right-hand at her and spoke up, "Bob Dylan..."

Midge reached out and vigorously shook his hand, "Nice to meet ya, Mr. Dylan. I'm Midge Galloway. You've got the same name as a folk-singer, did you know that? Now, who wants some of them thar Tay-cos?"

After the order was placed by phone, she was gone and we were back at our conference tables, reading, planning, and researching. This happened each day – Tex-Mex food for breakfast, lunch and dinner. El Chico's food was extraordinary. And Midge became equally dear to *all* of us – not just to Zack.

On the first and second days we prepared our plan for saving President Kennedy's life. As the de facto commander of this operation, Rick Besso was fastidious in his planning, as only a West Pointer and retired Lt. Colonel could be. He laid out the street map, the known facts of Oswald's actions, his perch, the sniper's nest, the angle of his firing – all the historical facts that came together to show us how the life of President Kennedy had been taken.

Then, he began presenting the details of the plan that would shift the focus directly on to the perpetrator in the 6th floor window of the Texas Book Depository at 411 Elm Street. Detail by detail, Rick presented the operation. We practiced the timing, the tone and volume of the voices.

Rick assigned duties and responsibilities to each of us. He purchased weapons and a bull-horn, walked us through the steps of where we would meet, where we do our duty and where we would re-meet upon the successful completion of keeping one man alive. Finally, we practiced a dress rehearsal for the pace of movements near where Zapruder would be filming. Telluric

Current One was just behind the grassy knoll area – an area that, Lord willing, no one would ever give a second thought to.

By November 20th, 1963, we were ready – which allowed us time to read more about the history that we had inadvertently moved, as one moves dominoes, creating newness all around us.

November 21st was when we each presented to the others in our group, what had happened in history. It was, as Zack and John Hay would say, a *mind-blower* for each of us, reading and sharing with our group a new past-world, a new future-order of that world, along with new names that had never meant anything to most of us in our past. Names like President Henry Wallace and President Alben Barkley surfaced in the 20th Century. The first woman elected to the U.S. Congress, Jeanette Rankin, became the first woman President.

Even stranger, were the men and women who surfaced in the 19th Century and displaced all those who had previously crowded the pages of history.

John Hay started it off, "President Hamlin emancipated all the slaves and worked with leaders, both black and white, to relocate all willing ex-slaves (who wished to leave the US), to the area of Panama, that in their time would be called Linconia. 3.9 million former slaves chose to relocate. A relatively small number (490,000) remained in the US and moved to the North." He paused, then continued.

"The Tycoon always believed in providing a 'new land' for freed slaves in which to resettle. It must have been one of the items that he and soon-to-be-President Hamlin agreed on. U. S. Senator Samuel C. Pomeroy, of the new state of Kansas, carried the bill and the U.S. Congress approved and funded it at the close of 1863, as one of the new president's landmark legislative victories."

"Legal segregation? Funded by the US Government and named after Lincoln – Linconia?" Louise asked. "*Are you kidding me?*"

"From my reading and the limited amount of discussion I had with him in the White House in 1861 and 1862, The Tycoon referred to it as 'separation'".

"Call it what you want, it's still unbelievable." Louise responded.

"And *sickening*." Zack added.

Hay, ever the supporter of Lincoln, proposed a different take on it. "I think that President Lincoln was a captive of his time's ideology. He said that he'd free all the slaves if it saved the Union *and that* he'd keep them in shackles if that action saved the Union."

"So..." Louise asked.

"So, after two years of fighting and dying between the rebels and the Union forces, my guess is that Lincoln and Hamlin decided to put their full weight of energy into pacification between the two races – and Linconia became their answer – and his trading piece with Hamlin."

We were shocked.

There were 31.4 million people in the United States at the time. So, a little over 12 percent of the entire population of Americans *left* America. Compare that to when the Revolutionary War was over and the British Loyalists left America, the number was only 80,000 which represented only about 3 percent of Americans who left America.

Rick said, "So, what happened?"

"Well, the exodus was initiated and certain black leaders rose to the head of it within the ex-slave community. While a number of former slaves did not join the exodus, they instead moved north and became highly successful; they were culturally embraced by those, particularly in Massachusetts and New England, who fought for the abolition of slavery. Those who left the country for Linconia became dual citizens, maintaining their newly acquired U.S. citizenship while also forging a new nation. One, in fact, was Mr. Willis Williams."

"The slave who aided the Union soldiers in capturing and killing the escaping ex-President of the Confederacy, Jefferson Davis?"

"That's the man. He became a hero to Linconia, to the ex-slaves, for what he did. Williams and his family relocated there with other key black leaders and helped guide the new nation to economic viability – and, as a minister of the Gospel, to a new Great Awakening. As years moved on, black missionaries were sent back to the continental U.S. and the new Great Awakening spread to whites.

Willis Williams became very successful and very wealthy in Linconia. He was also the one who helped build what *we* would have called The Panama Canal, *though* they actually named it after the President – The Hamlin Canal."

"And what about the great-grandson, Martin Luther King?" Rick asked.

"Oh, that's an interesting piece of history. Bear with me for a couple of minutes while I lay out the foundation, starting with King's great-grandfather, Mr. Williams."

"That's fine." Louise said.

Hay continued, "Willis Williams's son, Adam Daniel (A.D.) Williams was M.L. King's grandfather. He was born in 1863 at the end of the Civil War, just months before Gettysburg. As an infant, he moved with his parents to Central America at the end of that year, when Linconia was launched by President Hamlin."

"King's grandfather and great-grandfather?"

"Yes, correct. When Willis Williams, died in 1874, his son, A.D. Williams and his wealthy widowed mother returned to the U. S. – to Atlanta at first, as a part of that Christian missionary movement to whites and then soon moved to Massachusetts, where he grew to maturity, learned to preach at a young age, graduated from Harvard and married another ex-Atlantan, Jenny Parks, in 1891."

Putzi added, "Why do I feel like I'm hearing a genealogy from the Bible?"

We all chuckled.

Hay answered, "Because in a way, you *are* hearing that." He paused and then continued, "M.L. King's family members were like 'strangers in a strange land'; much like Abraham's family in the Torah."

Louise and Doc nodded. As Jews, they understood this reference about the namesake of Mr. *Abraham* Lincoln.

Hay looked down at his sheet of notes and continued, "It goes like this: Willis and his wife gave birth to A. D. in 1863, who in 1903 with his wife gave birth to sweet little Alberta, who grew up in Boston, fell in love with that ex-Atlantan and Harvard graduate, Michael King in 1926."

"Who's he?" I asked.

"Michael King is M.L. King's father." Hay answered.

"Wait, *what?* I thought his name was Martin Luther King, Sr... so that his son could be named Martin Luther King, Jr." I said.

"That's part of the interesting history I've stumbled on."

"Which is what?" Putzi asked.

"Well, Mike and Alberta King gave birth to a son on January 15th, 1929 and named him Michael "Mike" King, Jr.

"Where did the Protestant Reformer's name get inserted into this genealogy?" Putzi asked with a touch of German frustration.

"That's just it. It never *was* inserted. Apparently in the previous history, where Hitler reigned, King, Sr. went to Germany in 1934 and was impacted by the reformer, Martin Luther. However, in this alt-version of history, Hitler died in Café Central in 1913 and when Ernst Rohm became the leader of the Nazi movement in the 20's and 30's, the anti-Jewish and anti-black bigotry overwhelmed Germany and was much more dominant, disallowing visits to Germany by people of color from America and other countries, especially protestant American pastors." Hay said.

"So, Michael King, Sr. never went to Germany, never was impressed by the life of the reformer Martin Luther and never changed his name *or* that of his son. Am I correct?" I asked.

Doc interrupted the discussion, "Yes. As Mark Twain once wrote, about the German language 'You fall into error occasionally, because you mistake the name of a person for the name of a thing, and waste a good deal of time trying to dig a meaning out of it.' Maybe, just maybe, Michael King, Sr. never really needed to go to Germany – because his powerful preaching changed so many lives, beginning with his little son, Mike"

"Well said," Hay mentioned. "Little Mike became M.L. and grew up in Boston, graduated from Harvard, as did his father and grandfather and entered into both politics and ministry in Massachusetts, eventually developing young professional friendships with Jack and Bobby Kennedy, among others."

Having been quiet for some time, Jack Lewis spoke up. "May I update you all on the items I stumbled across? It's also rather unique."

We all nodded for him to continue.

"Well, to begin with, do you remember that beautiful young lady, Elizabeth Bacon, whom we met, walking with President Lincoln? Well, she eventually married her beau, George Armstrong Custer, the Boy General, and in short order, within a decade or so, became the First Lady of the United States."

We all looked at one another, as the reality set in.

"Indeed…Custer was nominated by the Democratic Party and elected President in 1876. He was barely old enough to serve, at 35 years old."

Doc looked at Jack with astonishment and spoke for all of us. *"What?"*

Jack added, "And that's not even the strangest of the things yet to be…"

44

The Bend of History Curves Unexpectedly

1963 Dallas

Jack Lewis had a way about himself that presented facts, ever so coolly.

"With Lincoln retired to Springfield, Illinois, President Hamlin ran for President in 1864 and beat Congressman Clement Vallandigham of Ohio."

I interrupted, "You mean the congressman that, in *our* previous history, Lincoln arrested and had the Union forces deposit on the Confederates' side, because he was so anti-Union? *That congressman*?"

Jack nodded and took a puff off of his pipe, smirked a bit and then added, "Yes, poor chap. Just seven years later after losing the Presidency and leaving Congress, he was arguing a legal client's innocence in court by showing how the victim had shot himself. As the records say "Demonstrating this possibility before the court with a gun he thought was unloaded, Vallandigham accidentally shot himself in the chest and died twelve hours later."

Zack winced and said, "Whoa, that brings a whole new meaning 'shooting your mouth off.'" No one responded.

Jack continued, "A new form of cultural division between and among whites-only began, New-South vs Old-South which took the place of white vs. black racism. With the movement of the black population to Linconia, economic racism filled the void. Hatred of one's brother seems to have no color limitation. Cain and Able, that sort of thing…"

He continued, opening a book on U. S. Presidents by the historian Dr. David Ripley, and reading from it, "'The list of presidents from 1860 on, reads as follows:

- Abraham Lincoln, 1861-1863
- Hannibal Hamlin, 1863 – 1869
- Gen. John Sedgewick, 1869 – 1877
- Gen. George Custer, 1877 – 1885

Doc reacted, "How in the world did that impetuous and uncontrollable Boy General become President?'

Again, without being dragged into the emotion of the moment, Jack Lewis calmly responded, "Because he didn't die."

Doc said, "How's that?"

Lewis, lighting his pipe again and brushing away the smoke as he exhaled, explained. "It seems that when the Civil War ended two years earlier, in 1863, than in our traditional history, U. S. Grant was deprived of the glory he would have had in 1865. Since there was no 'Hero of Appomattox Court House' accepting Lee's surrender, there was also no *President* Grant that was elected in 1868. Instead, the glory of the Union victory was focused on *General* John Sedgewick… er, I mean *President* John Sedgewick and his Secretary of State, the other hero of Gettysburg, The Boy General, George Custer, who was too young to be selected as Vice President. He'd have to wait eight years, until the calendar caught up with his age; when he'd turn 35 and the U.S. Constitution would allow him to run. He did so in 1876 and won, chiefly because of his Civil War record and the power of publicity generated by his wife, Libbie Custer. *She was a master at publicity.*"

Jack continued, "Most people don't realize that it was President U.S. Grant who (in our historical dimension) deeply disliked the flamboyant Boy General in the summer of 1876, Grant *did* approve Custer's request to re-join his troops at the Little Big Horn." Jack paused, "No Grant, no approval. No approval, no death. Instead, the summer of 1876 was Custer's moment in the political sun, winning the Democratic nomination and then the White House with the aid of his effervescent wife Libbie, whom we all met in 1863. She captured the attention of the American people unlike any other First Lady until Jaqueline Kennedy arrived at the White House fresh from the 1960 election of JFK. Custer's presidency was flamboyant and dramatic, but little else. A lot of gallantry, entertainment and glamor; a time of intellectualism and elitism."

Louise interrupted, "That's a big jump from Presidents in the mid-1870's to 1963. Who else served? Maybe I should ask, who were new and who never achieved the presidency?"

Jack Lewis, ever the college professor sat down at the table and handed out a list of names for his pupils to read. "Let's go backwards from JFK, so you can see how we arrived here, shall we?" Jack said as he approached the chalkboard that Midge had earlier secured for them and brought in to the room.

Jack began writing. "Before Kennedy – for eight years (1952-1960) was his mentor in the U.S. Senate, Alben Barkely."

Always the political trivia junkie, I asked "Wasn't he Harry Truman's Vice President? And what happened to Eisenhower? Did he get elected?" I added for good measure.

"*Yes*, to the first question about Truman's VP and *No* to the second one on Ike," he responded. "In the original history that we know, Barkley was Truman's V.P. for his final four years, but in this alt-history world, there was no 'President Truman'".

"*There was no Truman*, how do you mean?" I asked.

Jack explained, "In our *original* history Truman was Franklin Roosevelt's third and final Vice President. He only served 82 days before Roosevelt died in 1945 – just as Lincoln had two Vice Presidents and his second one, Andrew Johnson only served 42 days before Lincoln died. However, in *this* reality Lincoln lived and resigned; thus, Hamlin became President.

Well, sadly, FDR was assassinated by a deranged, unemployed brick layer, Giuseppe Zangara." Jack pulled out a research document and began reading.

"'On February 15th, 1944 FDR had just finished a speech in Miami's Bayfront Park from the back seat of a large convertible limousine. Zangara opened fire. From the six rounds expended, FDR was hit by five of them. He died in the arms of Anton Cermak, the Mayor of Chicago, who was travelling with him"

Jack continued, "Then-current Vice President Henry Wallace was sworn in as President. Wallace ran for President in 1944 and won. He served for eight years as an avowed socialist and brought America to a completely different destination than the happy days of *I Like Ike.* It was a terribly difficult economic time – a second Great Depression.

U.S. Senator Alben Barkley, Jack Kennedy's mentor, ran against Wallace and was elected in 1952, paving the way for JFK in 1960.

Harry Truman, was only ever *Senator* Truman. He served several more terms and retired."

"But what happened to General Eisenhower, *Ike,* becoming President Eisenhower?" I asked.

Lewis continued, with an odd noticeable historian's twinkle in his eyes. "There was no General Eisenhower, because there was never any West Point graduate named Eisenhower. He was medically discharged in his second year at the academy due to a football injury received when playing opposite the Olympic champion, Jim Thorpe." Jack picked up a biography entitled *Jim Thorpe's History of the Olympics.*

"Here it is; it was published in 1932."

He opened the book and read, "Thorpe attended Carlisle Indian School and played football for them. In 1912 his school gained a spot of the schedule to play Army Football at West Point. His athletic strength was well known and Cadet Eisenhower, along with his teammates, made plans to stop Thorpe and gain a level of athletic fame."

Jack looked at Rick and asked a question, "Was it normal for cadets who wanted to become famous, to hit high profile players like Thorpe and knock them out of the game – sending them to the hospital?"

Rick responded, "Maybe, I'm not sure but my guess is that if *we* tried to knock players out of the game, (as we tried with Tony Dorsett when Army played Pitt in 1975), Ike's team probably tried to nail Thorpe in 1912, as well."

Jack smiled, "American football – a chance to hit players extremely hard, all the while looking forward to visiting a pub with them afterwards for a pint! But in this case, your young 'Ike' Eisenhower had his plan backfire. He never visited a pub after his game. He was taken to the hospital. You see, the West Point linebackers attempted a 'savage' hit against 'the world's greatest athlete' early in the first quarter. Eisenhower and a classmate teamed up against the future Olympian, hitting him simultaneously as hard as they could. Thorpe went down, grabbing his shoulder, writhing on the ground. The cadets prematurely celebrated."

C.S. Lewis continued, as though he was telling the concluding pages of The Lion, The Witch and The Wardrobe. "You see, Jim Thorpe recovered almost immediately, and on a subsequent play he dodged Cadet Eisenhower and another Army linebacker, as they tried that same pincer-move against Carlisle's best. The Army linebackers both completely missed Jim Thorpe and smashed into one another. They, too, writhed on the ground and *they* did not get up." Jack laughed.

"They were removed from the game on stretchers. Carlisle beat Army 27-6. Jim Thorpe went on to the Olympics in Sweden and Dwight David Eisenhower went home to Kansas, medically discharged from West Point."

Jack summed it up, "So Eisenhower disappeared into history. That made the line-up:

- Franklin Roosevelt
- Wallace
- Barkley
- Kennedy

Jack paused and took a sip of tea that he'd prepared for himself. He cleared his throat and said, "From 1904 to 1932 there were eight presidential elections, from Teddy Roosevelt to Herbert Hoover. They remained the same, with only two exceptions."

Doc asked, "And who were those exceptions?"

Jack turned, so that he was now face-to-face with John Hay, and said calmly and coolly, "There were 15 times in the original history of the United States where the office of Vice President was left vacant by resignation, death or ascension to the Presidency because of presidential predecessor's death," Professor Lewis continued.

"To be specific, seven vice presidents died in office: Your President Madison had two Vice Presidents die in office during his two administrations: George Clinton and Elbridge Gerry.

Then there was William Rufus De Vane King (who served and died under Franklin Pierce), Henry Wilson (served and died under U.S. Grant), Thomas Hendricks (served and died under Grover Cleveland's first of two non-sequential Presidencies), Garret Hobart (served and died after only two years under William McKinley's first administration), James Sherman (later served and died under William Howard Taft). Two vice presidents resigned: John C. Calhoun and Spiro Agnew."

Again, Jack Lewis paused, took inventory of our attention to his teaching. We were dumb-struck. None of us knew these facts. Then, he delivered the final fact, along with lighting up that pipe of his and adding his Cheshire Cat smile, "The vice presidency has been vacant due to resignation or death a total of 37 years and 290 days, about a fifth of the time in history."

Putzi broke the silence and asked the obvious question, "Well then, who would have become President of the United States in each of those cases, had the President died, too?"

Jack answered, "Each time the line of succession made it available for another individual – since the office of Vice President would remain vacant – to be in the wings, should the sitting President die. Often it was the Secretary of State, though the line of succession was changed in 1947. Also, the ability to exercise the appointment of a Vice President to the vacant office didn't happen until 1967."

John Hay fully understood this reality in the original dimension. He had served as Secretary of State under two Presidents – McKinley and Teddy Roosevelt – when the office(s) of Vice President became vacant, each time. And each time, due to an 1886 law that placed the Secretary of State just behind the Vice President in the line of succession, John Hay was next in line… twice.

Hay stated matter of factly, "As I was next heir to the Presidency… they were both deeply fearful and troubling times for our nation. For my family and for me. I did *not* want to serve as President."

Jack continued, "Colonel, what you do not realize is that when one of those vacancies occurred, with the unexpected death of President McKinley's first Vice President, Garret Hobart in 1899, and you became next in line for the Presidency – in that alternate spacetime silo, Mr. McKinley died also, as a result of an early strain of the Spanish Flu; the pandemic that would later overwhelm the world two decades later – and you actually became President."

Hay stood silent, stunned.

"I, I, I don't know what to say." He sat down and slowly asked, "When did I serve?"

Jack continued, "For two years. You were President from 1899 to 1901. Then, Teddy Roosevelt ran for President and served 8 years, he asked you to return as Secretary of State."

Hay shook his head in disbelief, "I was President of the United States..."

"Yes, you were," Jack softly said.

Zack broke the moment, "You said there were two noticeable exceptions for the Presidency. Who was the other?"

Jack finished up on his historical discoveries, in this new reality "Yes, thank you young Mr. Besso. From Roosevelt to Roosevelt – *that is from Teddy to FDR* – the only other change in the presidency was that America gained its first woman President. Her name is Jeanette Rankin, from Montana – she was also the first woman to be elected to the U.S. Congress in 1914. She served only one term, since Woodrow Wilson chose her for his Vice President in 1916. Then Wilson died in the mustard gas attack by Ernst Rohm's Nazi invasion of America in 1918. President Rankin became a "war president' and negotiated with Germany for what was called the Long Peace. It was a terrible time and the subject of another discussion on another day." He took a deep breath.

Louise responded with a great gasp, "A woman president in 1918! That is remarkable, purely and utterly amazing."

Jack added, "It was the juggernaut force of the suffragette movement in America. Women voting changed the full force of politics in America under President Rankin."

He paused and then shifted gears, "That brings us up to date for the 20th Century... *and* about the possibility of saving President John F. Kennedy from the assassin's rounds."

Louise asked the hard question that we were all thinking, "Other than the sheer humanity of saving a President's life from a massive mortal gunshot wound, what is the historical significance of saving John F. Kennedy's life today?"

Jack Lewis massaged his palms together and said with a warm intensity, "Ah, there's the rub. I perceive that we all desire to keep the flow of history continuing past the year 2060 – the earliest time that Isaac Newton said the end of the world would occur. And we believe that in saving these leader's lives we will postpone the apocalypse. Am I correct?"

We all nodded.

C.S. Lewis, theologian, author, professor, widower and soon to be departed soul, smiled, lit his pipe once again, exhaled a cloud of fragrant pipe smoke and said, "What if we're wrong?"

45

Spacetime Travel – Flexible History but a Final Firm Result

1963 Dallas

It hardly seemed like a moment to eat, but Midge's timing, even as an interruption, had proven to be perfect. Her visits to El Chico were always on time and produced an array of delectable tacos, tamales, enchilada and other "Tex-Mex" meals.

"Tex-Mex" is what El Chico was becoming well-known for – a blending of traditional Mexican food along with flavorful blends from Texas – tastes that would ultimately capture the attention (and taste buds) of many Americans, when Six Flags over Texas grew – and people from throughout the U.S. flocked there, enjoying this new food – cooked by, you guessed it, El Chico.

"May I say a blessing over the food?" Midge bashfully asked.

Jack spoke for all of us, "Why certainly! That would be lovely."

Midge closed her eyes and in her soft Texan accent reverentially prayed, "Bless us, oh Lord, and these, thy gifts, which we are about to receive from thy bounty, through Christ, our Lord, Amen"

Instinctively, we all mirrored her last word and then dug into the excellent food.

Jack Lewis challenged us with his question, 'What if we're wrong' regarding our ability to change events and extend the time the Earth has left; before it eventually implodes in fire sometime after the year 2060, according to Isaac Newton.

So, it was at meal time that Doc began the cross-examination of C.S. Lewis as Tex-Mex aromas filled the air and in short order, gave way to serious people, seriously eating. The meal was simply superb.

"Jack, if I understand it correctly, your premise is that the flexibility of spacetime possibilities is anchored to the mathematically firm reality of end-time specifics. Is that right?" Doc said.

"Do you mean that 'all roads lead to Rome'?" Jack responded.

"How's that?"

"Do we wind up historically at the same place, no matter what? – is that what you're asking?" Jack continued without waiting for an answer, "Going back to your mathematical terms, do you hear me saying that, *as in any specific problem*, there are many formulaic possibilities, but they can only all lead to one answer… is that what you are asking?" Jack said.

Doc said, "Yes, I suppose so."

"All right, fair question. So, just as when you, Will, Louise and Putzi witnessed the deaths of Herr Hitler et al at Café Central, you also soon observed how human nature abhors a vacuum – and hence, Ernst Rohm rose in power and ruled the Nazis and misguided mankind sang out, 'Long live The Fuhrer'".

"Umm, The *Founder*, I think Rohm called himself The Founder," Doc responded. "And only the Germans felt that way."

Jack assisted him in that goal. "Again, point taken. 'Germany's Founder'... Allow me to answer your greater question in this fashion: When I was an atheist, I knew that bad people existed and I knew I wasn't one of them. Then, when I became a deist, those same *bad* people continued to exist, though I hoped I was not one of them. One might go to prison, yet another would take his place on the streets, hurting and stealing and so forth. In both cases I hoped it just wouldn't be me."

Zack added, "It's like Whack a Mole."

Jack looked at his young friend, "What? *Whack* a mole? What a dreadful name!"

Jack paused, "Have you no respect for Clodsley Shovel or any of the other talking moles or beasts of Narnia? They are intelligent animals. Smart little buggers who love peace."

Zack shook his head and responded, "*Whack a Mole.* It's a mechanical game where mole-heads pop up out of their holes. The player, at the ready, has a wooden mallet and tries to knock each mole in the head, as they pop up, and by doing so wins the game by the sheer number of successful head-bangings."

Jack looked incredulously at Zack. Shaking his head and yet smirking, as he walked back to his chair, he added, "I don't understand you."

Then, addressing the rest of us Jack said, "Then, when I became a Christian, I began to see that those around me were not just people who did bad things, but that they (and I) were somehow corrupted in our very nature. And that there were also spiritual entities behind mankind that did corrupt things – those entities that live in the shadowlands of mankind's life."

Louise's curiosity and interest in the subject forced her comments front and center. "Devils, demons, that sort of thing, right?"

Jack winced and responded, "Yes, those things, but *more* than those things."

Zack laughed, "How could there be *more* than devils and goblins and zombies?"

Jack looked at Zack, "Please, friend, there is no room yet for a *reductio ad absurdum* comment here, is there?"

Zack looked at the ground and quietly apologized.

Jack continued, "The greater issue, certainly at the core of deeply hurtful intentional behaviors – whether by man or by devil – is the understanding of a 'target that was missed.'"

"What?" Putzi asked sarcastically. "Why are we talking about a misfire in archery?" Jack looked at Putzi as a professor would look at an inattentive first-year college student. He responded with nothing, as he turned back to Doc and brought the topic again into focus.

"Traditional orthodoxy tells us that Man and Woman came into existence by a Creator, a father." He took a sip of water from the tumbler. "Just as every father *or mother* desires happiness for their children…" he paused. Then he interrupted himself, "Hold on, that's quite a unique word, 'desire' – the Latin roots implying 'from the stars or constellations' – every father and mother *on Earth* desire their children to live a good life, a safe life and for them to shoot their arrow to the stars; so does the Creator *of* those stars. From that dimensional perch to way beyond the stars and constellations He desires the *best* for us."

He paused, adjusted his gaberdine trousers as he sat in the large, comfortable chair, and took a puff on his pipe, "That particular *best* was polluted *or corrupted* at some point. As Josephus writes in his *Jewish Antiquities*, 'At that time, all living creatures spoke a common language, and a serpent maliciously lured the woman into tasting of the tree of wisdom, promising a blissful existence equal to that of a god.'"

Putzi couldn't hold back, "Oh, Jacksie, please do not embarrass yourself by turning to fables and folklore. Animals talking! Such foolishness!"

Jack smiled, "Argue with Josephus, not with me!' He paused, his eyes twinkling even more, "Maybe even argue with Aslan, too, which would in fact prove Josephus's comment, I suppose."

Putzie asked, "Who?"

Jack responded, "Never mind. What I *do* know is that something in our DNA changed when the first parents of humanity broke with their father. They were disinherited, in a sense. Their 'best' was polluted and they eventually died. Originally, the Creator desired – *there's that word again* – for them to never die. They misfired as they attempted to shoot for the stars."

He added, "Oh, and Herr Putzi, when an archer misfires at an intended target ring, it is said that he 'sins'... which I think is a clever way of explaining a fully terrible concept when mankind misses the mark, don't you?"

Putzi thought about it for a second and then nodded.

Jack stopped and looked at our group of spacetime travelers and asked, "Does death even make sense? Don't we all feel deep down that we were born to live forever? Yet, we die."

Jack Lewis continued, "Sin birthed death, which in turn hurt us. It is our own miscarriage, at birth, stopping us from living forever. It's brought about by corruption, which stopped so much 'life' – and still stops so much life each day. Even as we – we small band of siblings – travel through space and time and see so many options, so many roads down which we could travel to Rome or Egypt – so many theorems and postulates that are used to still arrive at only one accurate solution for living forever."

Doc finally reacted, "And accurate solutions are that *first*, the Earth will end and *second,* we will all die? My God, how utterly depressing."

Jack responded, "You err in your understanding. More accurately, the correct order is that *first*, most of us will die and *second,* the Earth will pass away. The order is important to understand. And Isaac Newton said that the year 2060 would be important in its passing. He made this statement prior to own his death, about an event that would be three hundred years in the future. He understood the importance of the order of those questions, for all of mankind's sake."

Doc asked, "So why in the world have we, *have I,* been so busy in spacetime travel, saving the lives of millions, by seeing those who perpetrate evil depart sooner rather than later, when we're all – *they're all* – going to die anyway? And why were we in Washington D.C. with Lincoln in 1863 and why are we here now in Dallas in 1963, attempting to stop the death of another President of the United State of America?"

Doc was agitated.

Jack turned his pipe upside down and tapped out the ashes onto a small smoking tray. "Dr. Gersema, you pose a very brilliant and profound series of questions."

"Thank you. *And...*?" asked Doc, as if waiting for the other shoe to drop.

Author C. S. Lewis looked deeply into Doc's eyes as he brought his final remarks to bear on the leader of our spacetime travelers. "This world is not your permanent home. It's more like a tent. And, like a tent it needs to be attended to, to be swept clean when needed and to be mended when ripped."

Jack Lewis turned to us and added, "That's our job. We all, *here assembled,* have been given the honor of mending the many temporary dimensions of time and space – eleven, correct?"

Doc responded, "Well, more accurately, ten dimensions plus time – so, yes, eleven. Those ten dimensions give us ten Telluric Currents. We've yet only used one, Telluric Current One."

Jack continued, "...We've been given the honor of seeing evil stopped, displaced and otherwise mitigated. The tent swept clean and mended. And just as that terrible game that you like to play, Zack, what's it called – 'Whack a Mole'?"

Zack, "Yep, that's the name."

"Just like Whack a Mole, the evil inherent in family lines and their progeny continues to pop up – over and over again. It is systemic, it hurts deeply and yet… contrary to what it feels like, there is hope. The Creator, the father, has written himself into the story of mankind. One singular act of mercy paid the price. For us, one act of kindness at a time remains all we can do in the broad expanse of time and space to both accept such unmerited favor and to thank him. We must remain vigilant each day, while we are still here, still alive. Like Newton, we must be aware of what's in front of us this day, while we plan to help others; those not yet born."

Rick intentionally interrupted, "No offense, Jack, but today is November 21st, 1963 – tomorrow is the day that cries out for us to change history, for the one life of John Fitzgerald Kennedy."

Rick looked at all of us, "Are we still going through with our plan to save President Kennedy's life? Does that remain a priority amid this discussion of hope and hopelessness?"

There was no hesitancy in the entire group, despite the rather sobering theological lecture by which Jack had just challenged us.

"Yes," we all responded.

Jack's response was the loudest.

46

November 22nd

1963 Dallas Twelve Thirty pm

November 22nd 1963. Dealey Plaza, Dallas, Texas.

It unfolded right before our eyes.

According to plan, Doc and John Hay stepped off of their respective curbs along Houston St. and began delivering their lines, yelling, pointing up at the sniper's nest.

The cacophony of sound, motion and action on the curb made the responses by the Secret Service agents accelerate rapidly. All eyes in the crowd were now looking directly at the open window on the corner of the 6th floor of the Texas Book Depository Building. The sniper's face and upper torso were clearly visible.

Lee Harvey Oswald had just swung his 6.55 mm Mannlicher-Carcano rifle from its former original perch directly up at the motorcade on Houston Street, straight into the face of the President of the United States. Putzi had Oswald in his sights; he squeezed off two rounds to Oswald's head, just as a chorus of other rounds from the ground-level joined in.

The Chief Agent of the President's Secret Service detail, Clint Hill, threw himself over the back of the Lincoln limousine and covered the Kennedys with his body. Governor Connally and his wife were covered by another agent.

The Presidential motorcade took an immediate and forceful left onto Elm St. in front of a book depository building and raced to the Stemmons Freeway on-ramp without further incident. Jack Kennedy was alive.

Another young person, a woman, lay at the base of the building, fatally shot. Librarian Midge Galloway had come to see the President on a whim to possibly see a male friend, along with a fellow librarian; they were standing on the sidelines of the motorcade in front of the Texas Book Depository Building. A stray round ended her life.

She was now dead, yet alive in eternity; the President of the United States was alive now but would still one day die. Jack Lewis would also die today in 1963, and like young Midge, he would become truly alive.

But not yet.

Twelve minutes later, as our group met at a predetermined spot – tucked behind the now-*un*important grassy knoll, John, Doc, Jack, Louise, Putzi, Rick and Zack all walked together with me as made our way to the adjacent Telluric Current One. Jack withdrew a card with his own signature on it. Next to his autograph was printed "The Kilns, 1938".

We knew it was time for Jack Lewis to leave us.

He said to us, "Dear friends, I must return to my writing in that upstairs home-office, where you met me. You invited me on this journey and I accepted. Where we went is beyond science, far beyond science fiction."

Doc spoke for all of us, "Jack, you have impacted us all. Your work on *The Silent Planet* eclipses H.G. Wells' work, it really does."

Jack nodded in appreciation and responded, "Thank you, but my concern is how in the world I will be able to have my four young children's journey to Narnia mirror even a portion of what we have accomplished on our journeys here."

Putzi added, "Herr Lewis, I have a thought for you."

"Yes, Putzi, what is it?"

"I know you're struggling for their names. I suggest you make it easy by making them all boys."

Jack looked at him, expecting additional comments to come his way.

Putzi waited, then looked at Zack, "Ja, I think that the names should be John, Paul, George and Ringo."

Zack laughed out loud, exactly the response I think Putzi was hoping for. We followed Zack's lead.

Jack chuckled, "I'll take that under advisement, but rest assured one name that will definitely find its way into my list of animal characters in whatever story I tell, will be Putzi the Little Piggy!"

We all laughed and hugged Jack Lewis. John Hay thanked Jack profusely. "You are a man of faith, a man of integrity and a man who has taught me not to fear death, but to engage in the life that God has given us, until it is right for us to join him – not by accident, but because it's our distinct time to leave this world.

Jack responded, "Colonel, you have walked with giants yet I sense that you now need to sit with family. Your son and your wife need you. Clara will live until 1914. You need her. You never needed power. You only needed love. Why don't you return to Springfield for the final years of your life, start a summer colony for your group of friends, reconnect with Mr. Lincoln and regain what truly are all the best prizes in life, including a love of God.

The Colonel hugged Jack and said "I will."

Louise spoke for all of us, "Jack, live well, love deeply and write outside of time and space. The world will always need C. S. Lewis and the silos of space and time from which your wonderful stories are sent."

He placed his own right palm on the card which held the name of his residency and the year 1938, stepped onto Telluric Current One and was gone.

John Hay next stepped up to the Telluric Current, needing nothing further to say, unfolded a letter from his wife, dated 1869, from Springfield. He nodded to us, placed his hand on her signature and in a swoosh of sound was immediately back in the Land of Lincoln – walking up to a table at which sat Clara and former President Lincoln, now 60 years old. John Hay beamed, and said, "Mr. President"; Lincoln looked up and smiled, extending his hand to the man who walked with giants.

Next in Dallas to depart were Rick and Zack Besso. They stepped up to Telluric Current One. Rick said, "Well folks, it's time for the Besso Brothers to return to the Vienna of 1913. Thank you, Doc, for allowing us to join you on this adventure." Turning to me, Zack said, "Will Clark, you and Jack Lewis have given us much to think about regarding Isaac Newton's theory of the year 2060."

Rick added, "It's a lot to take into our minds, but then again, so is spacetime travel. Somehow the works of mankind's hands tend to trick us into thinking that we are more creative than even the one who made us. On that point, I have since moved a position – because of men of faith like you and Jack. Thank you."

I shook both men's hands, then the other members of our group, Doc, Louise and Putzie hugged them."

Doc said to his friends – to *our* friends – "Dear Besso Brothers, our paths may well cross again, either in Vienna or elsewhere, and know that when they do, your *wildness* will always be near and dear to our hearts."

Tears welled up in all of our eyes.

Zack surprised us all by pulling out a handbill with an autograph on it. "We're not headed to 1938 but we're going to 1983."

Putzi asked, "What's in 1983?"

"U2."

"What… you want me to go with you?" Putzi asked.

"No," said Zack. "U2, not *you, too*...We haven't invited you. We're headed to a rock'n'roll festival... and *Ringo's* not going to be in it."

Putzi said, "Why did you say, 'You too'? Wait, you both are headed to a music festival, and who's playing at it?"

"U2." Rick responded, egging along his confusion.

"I am?" asked Putzi, "But you said I wasn't going with you to the festival. Or did I misunderstand something?"

Zack looked at his German friend and said, "Putzi, you are a fabulous musician on the piano, correct?"

"Yes, and accordion."

Rick gagged, "Um, yeah, that's not a good recommendation, my friend."

"Oh, sorry," Putzi added. "Yes, I am an experienced pianist and have played for years in Germany and in America. I played for President Teddy Roosevelt at the White House"

Rick looked at Zack and smiled, then said, "Well, that's a whole lot better than oom-pah music. Would you like to go to an US Festival?"

"Don't you mean *with* us to a festival?" Putzi asked.

"No," Zack corrected him again, "Would you like to go to the *US* Festival in 1983 and hear some incredible rock music?"

Rick pointed to the autograph on the handbill Zack held, smiled and said, "I have a friend from the military, Col. Willis Herbert "Woody" Wood, who helped construct the concert venue in Southern California – Glen Helen Park in San Bernardino. His autograph can get us there by Telluric Current One; he can get us into the concert. *Woody* loves to spacetime travel with Zack and me, so we'll probably take him someplace after it, as a 'thank you'."

Zack added, "The co-founder of Apple Computers, Steve Wozniak, is bringing together incredible acts like Van Halen, Ozzie Osbourne and... *U2*. Oddly enough, in the future the Los Angeles Times will call it 'The Music Festival that time forgot.' But not us, my little German Sausage!"

Putzi laughed, glanced over at Doc, Louise and me with a quizzical look on his face, as if to say *'Should I?'*

We each mouthed 'Do it!'

The three men held onto the handbill and stepped onto Telluric Current One.

In a moment, in the twinkling of an eye, The Besso Brothers and Ernst 'Putzi" Hanfstaengl were absent from the grassy knoll and present with The Edge, Bono and U2. They were embraced by the lyrics of the song, Gloria: *"Gloria, in te domine, Gloria, exultate. Oh Lord, if I had anything, anything at all, I'd give it to you, I'd, I'd give it to you."*

Section XIII

47

Stayin' Alive

1977 Southern California

Louise, Doc and I knew that we must relocate to the near future, but securing how we would accomplish it was lost on us. None of us prepared by bringing autographs, signatures or DNA to move us from 1963 to the immediate future in the 70's or 80's. We *did* have DNA set aside for the 21st Century. We three knew we would proceed towards 2060, but we had nothing to land us in the 70's or 80's.

That is until something clicked in my mind. Or better yet, in my wallet.

A 1977 faded, but still beautiful, snapshot of my bride on our wedding day was tucked in the right side of my well-worn brown wallet. I'd carried that wallet for decades. My sweet Carole died of cancer in 2009.

On the back of the photo, in her writing, was written, "To my husband, my love. Yours always, Love ya, Carole."

I paused as I thought about what we might attempt. It could look selfish, incredibly selfish, though I hoped it wouldn't be.

I turned to Louise and Doc, "It's just the three of us now and I have an idea," I said.

Louise and Doc looked at each other, then looked at me. "Go ahead," Doc said.

"There are two absolutes about the current history before us," I said. "First, before we head towards 2060, we must go to 1977 and see how we've affected America."

Louise nodded, then quietly asked, "And the other absolute?"

I looked at them and said matter-of-factly, "I want to see my wife alive – from afar – one last time. It would be during our first year of marriage."

Louise and Doc questioned me further on my intent. With each question I was relaxed and assured them that I would not interfere with the marriage of my younger self and my bride.

I suppose in some ways it was a quid pro quo; the only document with DNA on it that could secure our passage way to the late 1970's was what I held in my pocket and they would have to trust me. I had no ill intent and I hoped they saw that in me.

"Alright, let's do it," Doc said. I opened my wallet, withdrew Carole's picture, turned it over and the three of us placed our hands on her writing as we stepped onto Telluric Current One. The next thing we heard were the Bee Gees singing *Stayin' Alive.*

48

Catching Up on History

1977 Los Angeles Area

We were now just outside of Los Angeles in a small city called West Covina. It was the late autumn of 1977.

Doc, Louise and I were standing in the lobby of the Sunset Manor apartments, the rental complex in which Carole and I first experienced married life. Someone else was retrieving mail from the personal mail boxes in the lobby. He had a transistor radio tuned to a Los Angeles radio station playing the Bee Gees' hit single *Stayin' Alive*, for what was probably the *five hundredth* time that day.

My reactions surprised me as I was so quickly thrust back into my past, the sights, sounds and smells of apartment living all around us. In the center of the complex was, what I used to consider, an extremely large swimming pool – the size of which I had never seen until we moved in. Memories came flooding in. All good. All sweet.

There was also a soberness.

From my current perspective, the pool somehow looked smaller, the complex looked like every 1970's-built apartment building I'd seen over the decades in our lives as mortgage company owners, land owners and residential homeowners.

The whole apartment complex looked smaller, starker. Perspective changes even in spacetime, maybe especially in spacetime. As Paul Simon once wrote, "Everything looks worse in black and white."

We turned to exit the lobby and head toward a place we could quickly read about what had happened in history. Not too terribly far away was the San Gabriel Valley Tribune. We determined to investigate this version of alt-history from 1963-1977 in that publisher's archive.

Doc, Louise and I called a cab and began the investigation as soon as the cabbie pulled his vehicle to the curb and welcomed us in. We gave him the name of our destination.

"The Tribune, now that's a good paper. I've subscribed to that for years. They hate ALL politicians," said the smirking cabby.

"How long have you been a cabbie?" I asked.

"Oh, ever since '73, I suppose, he answered.

"What did you do before '73?" I followed up.

"Oh, I was a mortgage banker – I helped fund money for new home-owners"

Doc chimed in, "*Really,* did the financial market go bad?"

The cabby said, "Where you been, pal? Of course, it did. That Kennedy sure had it hard. I betcha *he's* glad he was only in for one-term. The interest rates went sky high, just like prices. We're still recovering."

Louise asked, "President John F. Kennedy?"

"No, I'm talking about his little brother, Bobby. What a mess he had to deal with! After JFK, President Mike King was elected in '68 – and did a decent job for a guy who had only previously been a preacher and a civil rights leader. He brought the nation further together, I suppose. Even dual citizens from Linconia moved back to the United States and voted for King."

The cabby veered left onto a parkway and continued talking.

"President King also only lasted one term and went back to preaching. But holy cow, King's Vice President, Bobby Kennedy, got elected as President in '72 and he chose a state senator from Alabama or Georgia or someplace south. A guy named Carter."

Doc asked, "*Jimmy* Carter?"

"Yeah, that's him. It made my wife and me laugh."

"How so?" Louise asked.

"Oh, I don't know, just the names, 'Bobby and Jimmy'. We felt funny saying their first names. It just seemed too informal."

The cabby finished his political dissertation, "But then came our new president and inflation just shot through the roof – house roofs and car roofs."

The cabby turned his taxi car into the parking lot of the Tribune newspaper, "Well, we're here. That'll be $79 dollars for 7 minutes."

Doc choked a little bit, "$79?"

The cabby said "Well, it just turned $80…so I'm perfectly ok if you want to sit here and debate more as my taximeter spins like a fan and provides air conditioning for me. It's your call. That'll be $81 now."

We jumped out of the taxi like it was on fire and Doc threw 4 twenties and a dollar bill at our fast talking, fast driving, fast charging mortgage-banker-cabby and held his hand out for the change.

We stepped into the lobby of the San Gabriel Valley Tribune and met a young lady who showed us to the newspaper's archives, complete with the smell of ten thousand archived newspapers and seven huge microfiche machines, turned on and emitting a lot of heat, light and sound.

She excused herself and the three of us began our tasks that spanned from 1963 to 1977 – literally immersing ourselves in yesterday's news. Doc was charged with gathering U.S. political news, Louise was tasked with gathering European news and I focused in on economic trends – each of us reviewing 14 years of news from when JFK was given a new lease on his life.

49

Researching the New Past

1977 West Covina, CA

Fourteen years in "newspaper measurements" mean just over 5,100 daily and Sunday editions. An edition in 1977 ranged from three or four sections, each with 8 or so pages in them. That put a paper's length in those days at just around 30 pages per day. Enough info for a man or a woman to take time each morning or evening to sit and read the happenings of the day and then move on with their lives.

We had fifteen thousand-plus pages to peruse, grab headlines, dig down whenever possible and then reemerge from the data flood of new history to compare notes with each other. Doc and I had context with the 70's news and trends, Louise was a woman out of time, a stranger in a strange land, born and educated in the *early* 20th century. Nonetheless, she was an avid researcher and an amazing data-miner for any point in time. We three separated from one another and reconnected at increments to compare notes and share changes. Lunch was one of those times. Eventually, our stomachs pumped the brakes for lunch.

Near the newspaper was an In-n-Out Hamburger shack – thankfully one of the few things in our spacetime journey, that apparently was still the same.

We broke for lunch at In-n-Out and sat at an outside table with one of the familiar red and white sun umbrellas shading us as we ate and talked.

"So, let me get this straight," I asked Doc and Louise. "When we saved JFK's life in Dallas, he went on to win his reelection in 1964. Who'd he run against?'

Doc answered, "Governor George Romney of Michigan. He was a moderate Republican and President Kennedy presented a far more polished tone in his speeches and policies. What slaughtered Romney was his belief that we should engage deeper in a war in Vietnam. Kennedy withdrew the limited number of troops and advisers in 1965 and that little country fell to the communists. Romney attacked Kennedy as a coward, but the fact that Jack Kennedy was a bona fide Navy war hero from the previous war, while Romney remained a civilian and a car executive in Detroit during the war, hurt him badly. What 'did him in' towards the end of the election, was when Romney changed his position on Vietnam and said that the military brass had "brainwashed" him about supporting a war there."

"What a mess, yet Kennedy won."

"Overwhelmingly." Doc said.

"Did JFK keep Lyndon Johnson as his Vice President?" I asked.

"Nope. The Associated Press articles repeatedly said that Kennedy wanted more youth and vigor on the ticket so he picked the Reverend M.L. "Mike" King, who at 35 years old, filled the bill. Since King and Kennedy were both from Massachusetts, and the US Constitution doesn't allow a president and vice president to be residents of the same state, King had to quickly move, which he did. He moved his residency to Georgia, the home of his grandfather and great-grandfather. Sort of like what Dick Cheney did when George W. Bush selected him. Both were originally from Texas."

"Where'd Johnson go?"

Doc laughed, "He went back to Texas and into the pages of history, I suppose. I really didn't see him again in the news. The last photo I did see of him was with shoulder length long hair. The Atlantic Monthly said that he didn't want to look like the politicians in Washington D.C. anymore."

"So that's how King had a step-up to run for President in 1968! That makes sense." I paused, "What about Bobby Kennedy? Our opinionated cabby said that JFK's brother ran and won in '72. How did RFK and King avoid assassination when they each ran?"

Doc responded, "For King it was a simple matter of smoking inside, rather than outside"

What?"

Doc said, "Well, here's the story I found. Let me look at my notes." He paused and then continued. "In April of '68 King was speaking across Tennessee and stopped for the night with his campaign at Loree Bailey's motel in Memphis - The Lorraine Motel. King was a smoker. Not a lot of people knew that at the time. The photographers and press people liked King (and what he stood for) and knew that smoking was less and less acceptable to Americans in the late 60's and early '70's, so photos weren't taken of him indulging in his habit. That gave him a certain freedom and he'd go outside of hotel rooms and smoke. Apparently, that was the case in *our* history when he stepped outside of his room on April 4th, 1968 and James Earl Ray fired a headshot that killed the civil rights activist, M.L. King. Loree Bailey, the owner, was down below him on the first floor, by the manager's office, taking a smoke break, herself. She looked up at the sound of the gunshot and witnessed King's assassination. In response to it, she fell to the ground with a stroke and died within the hour. It seems Ray's round killed two people, not just one."

"But this wasn't *our* history." I added.

"Correct, in this alt-history case, with King as a possible Vice President and the press being less kind to a possible political candidate, he apparently ran out of cigarettes on the morning of April 4th, 1968, sent for a member of his campaign staff to buy some in the lobby of the Lorraine Motel from Loree Baily, the owner. She told the aid that Rev. King could "go ahead and smoke inside his room".

"So, he smoked, not out in full view of an assassin's rifle scope. And he lived, as did Loree Bailey. King became Vice President in '64 and then was elected President in '68." Doc paused, then added, "Who would have thought that smoking could both kill you *and* save your life?' I laughed out loud.

"Amazing," Louise said. "And Bobby Kennedy?" she added.

Doc took a bite from his Double-Double hamburger, then a sip of lemonade from the In-n-Out cup, added some fries and continued, "Now, this one is equally as interesting. Since Bobby Kennedy stood aside for King in 1968 and did not run for President himself, King was appreciative and asked him to be his Vice President with the idea, apparently, that when King was done, Bobby would receive King's support and endorsement in either '72 or '76."

I added, "So the bumper stickers and signs said, 'Kennedy-King' in '64 and then 'King-Kennedy' in '68?"

"Yep."

"And the country overwhelmingly voted for these three men, in their differing roles, over eight years?" I asked.

"More than that; the entire *decade* of the 1960's was the Kennedy Decade, in one form or another. King was instrumental in what the Kennedys wanted and he received from them what he wanted."

"Amazing," Louise said again.

Doc turned to Louise, "Well tell us what you found."

Louise wiped the corners of her lips with a napkin and took a final gulp from her chocolate milkshake, as she prepared to give an overview of her time in the newspaper stacks and microfiche.

"Well, international politics didn't fair so neatly nor so organized."

"What do you mean?" I asked.

"To begin with, "After John Kennedy's speech in Berlin in June of 1963, when he spoke those words "Ich bin ein Berliner… ugh, meaning *I am a Berliner*"

I interrupted her, "Oh yeah, don't you mean when he *misspoke* those words? Germans knew that the term 'ein Berliner' was a jelly-filled donut and the international press had a field day with mocking him because his audience laughed…"

It was Louise's time now to interrupt me, "No, Will, you are incorrect. As it turns out in Berlin, that particular donut is called a pfannkuchen and no one would have confused Kennedy's meaning, even using the word 'ein' in front of Berliner, as an indefinite article. My reading of the event shows that after Kennedy spoke the phrase in German, the translator *then* said the exact same thing in German and the President, who always had a quick wit, Kennedy thanked the translator for his accuracy in speaking German. The crowd roared at that point."

"I stand corrected," I sheepishly mumbled.

Doc added, "So what instabilities in international politics did you uncover?"

Louise started in. "Well, they all involved times when national leaders arrived for international events, starting with Winston Churchill's funeral in 1965. The former Prime Minister died at 90, ten years after his second go-round as PM. The funeral lasted four days and had been planned for a dozen years."

"A dozen years?" I asked.

"Yes, newspapers prepare obituaries far in advance for world leaders, even during my time in the early twentieth century;

they're ready for use at the drop of a hat... or the drop of a world leader."

Doc laughed out loud.

Louise smiled and continued, "Print publishers prepared one in 1953 that they retrieved with each of Churchill's seven strokes, until it was updated and *really* needed in 1965," she said.

"On the final day of the funeral ceremony, over 110 world leaders represented their countries. After the service, as the body of the twice-selected former Prime Minister was taken to its final resting place, the leaders waited for their limousines in the January cold. That's when someone attempted to detonate a claymore mine in the rear of the crowd directed at of the leaders. Later, it was determined that the failed global assassination was because of Churchill's long-held support for the birth of Israel," Louise said.

"Middle-east terrorists?" I asked.

"No one ever knew nor could they find out who did it – just that it involved Israel's right to exist – *or not*. From what I read, it was terribly frightening for the leaders – older leaders like Israel's former Prime Minister David Ben-Gurion, as well as young leaders, like the newly inaugurated team of Kennedy and King. The claymore did not detonate. The leaders were swept back into the cathedral by their respective protection details, who in time quickly worked together to extract them. This may have been the first example of a complete global group assassination."

Louise added, "Communism and the fledgling Cold War took a back seat throughout the 60's and 70's to the escalating situation in the Middle East."

"This scene was repeated several times with larger payloads throughout the years between '65 and '77. Complete global terrorism. The Olympics in '68, '72 and '76 were marred so deeply that world leaders refused to attend any large group setting, including sporting events and inauguration ceremonies of different world leaders. The United Nations shrunk into the background, refusing to condemn the acts. The terrorists even attacked during the World Cup and the World Championship of Football, several times during the 70's," Louise summed up.

"The World Championship of Football? Do you mean the Super Bowl?" I asked.

Not having ever read anything about the term 'Super Bowl', Louise's face went blank.

"I don't know what that was, but in this dimension, there's no such event named that."

I looked oddly at Doc and he returned the same expression.

"Ok, no Super Bowl..."

She continued, "The anti-Israel forces coalesced into a huge terrorist economic block and began causing citizens from the whole globe to be worried about even attending anything for sports, entertainment or travel/touring."

I asked, "Especially travel to Israel and the Middle East?"

Louise nodded *yes,* "The intensity of hatred against Israel was unbelievable, year after year," Louise said.

"And who's leading these efforts against Israel?" I asked.

Louise blanched, almost vomiting as she looked at us.

"It's Germany's Ernst Rohm..." she said.

"The Founder of Nazi-ism?" I asked.

"The monster is still alive," Louise said flatly.

50

Rohm Still Lives

1977

We walked back to the newspaper offices and returned to the room that had been set aside for us. I gave a thorough debrief to Doc and Louise on what I'd read regarding the financial markets and the movement by the European Common Market's efforts to strangle Israel's national finances.

It was painful to read about the racism and negative reactions to Jews and Israel, even more painful to detail it to my two Jewish friends.

I pushed ahead, "Somehow, after 1964, the United Nations and the European Common Market made joint policies accusing Israel of purposely undermining Europe's economy. Louise, until *you* put the pieces together about Germany's secretive financial leaders being connected to Ernst Rohm, *I* hadn't put together the pieces to the overall puzzle."

She said, "I was so stunned, myself, that he was alive and involved in this dimension, Will." Louise continued, "I could only find in the newspapers that when the Great Peace was negotiated, Rohm successfully negotiated with UN leaders for his own 'retirement'."

"How old is this tyrant?" Doc demanded.

"He was born in 1887, so he's 90 today, in 1977," I answered.

Louise added, "And he resides in the UN's Sanctuary City of Palm Springs, California. Lives like a king, it seems. Just as we saw his life before, in the first alt-history review of Rohm replacing Hitler."

"My God," Doc said, as he sat down and placed his head into his two palms, "This can't be true."

Louise looked at Dr. Russ Gersema, placed her hand on his shoulder and said, "In this dimension, although he obviously hates Jews and equally hates Israel, there are no indications of concentration camps and Holocaust murders of mass scale. At least not yet…"

I asked, "Who's his second in command?"

She paused and looked down at her notes, "It appears that it's a man named Balder von Schirach, from Vienna. He was the head of the Nazi Youth. He's in his late 60's."

Doc said, "Not quite a 'youth leader' right? But at least we know he'll be the next in line, when Rohm dies."

"When will that be?" I asked Louise.

Doc looked at Louise, as well.

She looked at both of us, "He just doesn't *ever* seem to die."

51

Till There Was You

1977

As the day concluded, we hailed a cab and made our way back to Sunset Manor, my apartment when Carole and I were first married. From there, we'd use Telluric Current One and exit out of 1977 and slingshot to 2060.

As we pulled up, I paid the cabby, whose opinions we didn't solicit. Our business here was completed.

Departing the cab, we walked into the lobby. I had hopes of seeing Carole but knew that my hope would probably not be fulfilled.

"Do you want to knock on the door of your old apartment and see if she answers?" asked Louise. I shook my head *No.*

Doc gave me a knowing side glance that seemed to re-ask the same question.

"Well, my agreement with you both was that I'd look at Carole from afar, not knock on our apartment door," I answered. "I don't want to upset my bride or our earlier life together."

I was in error.

Just as I said those words, the double glass doors opened from the apartments surrounding the large pool area and in walked Carole Clark, the bride of my youth and my wife whose life would end so many years later in the next century. She was fiddling with her keys as she walked past us toward the mailbox area for the apartments, whistling her then-favorite song 'Till There Was You.'

Louise and Doc backed up as I automatically moved towards Carole, saying nothing.

She turned and looked at me, embarrassed a bit, "Oh, I'm so sorry, sir. I didn't know you were there. I was in my own world, whistling away."

I responded, "It's a pretty tune. In fact, that's one of my favorite songs, as well." I paused, blown away at talking to my young bride. "Few people know that the Beatles covered that tune from The Music Man."

"I love their version; it was sung at my wedding by a friend." she said and paused. "On the Beatle's album, John Lennon's harmony with Pete Best and Stu Sutcliffe is so *very* beautiful." She paused, then added, "Are you here to see a relative… a son or daughter or some grandkids?"

I chuckled, "Nah, I'm here to see someone else, someone I also *do* dearly love." I just kept looking at her as she opened her mailbox, extracted the junk mail and a couple utility bills.

"Oh, that's lovely," she said a bit distracted as she perused the envelopes.

I added, "No checks?" and laughed.

She chuckled, as well, and lowered her arm holding the envelopes; she looked directly into my eyes and blinked.

"No checks." She continued looking at my body and my face. *"Have we met before, sir?"*

I smiled, not knowing exactly what to say, "Well, we might have. I've been in here more than a few times – getting mail for my family."

"Really?' Carole said. She was honestly intrigued and looked even further into my face.

"You *do* look familiar!" my wife said to me.

I responded, "I can tell you that if I had the honor of being friends with you and your husband, I'd be the luckiest of all visitors here at Sunset Manor."

Carole bored into my eyes and moved toward me, after hearing the rhythm and tone of my voice. "How did you know I have a husband?"

I knew this woman. I knew her nuances. I knew she was a skeptical elementary school teacher by profession, questioning every little student that ever sat in her class. Always looking for correct answers.

And I knew myself. I pointed my right index finger at my left wedding ring finger. "You mentioned that the Beatle song was sung at your wedding."

I tilted my head and smiled.

She blushed in the apologizing sort of way she always had.

"Oh, again, I'm so sorry, Mr…?"

I smiled again, reached out to shake her hand and immediately made up a name. "I'm Nathan Colin."

As she reached out to shake my hand, she dropped a couple pieces of mail on the floor. I reached down, picked them up and returned them to her.

"That's a very nice name," she said.

Knowing that those were the first names of our future two sons, I was pleased by her response. I let her response hang in the air, as I shook her hand, even placing my other hand on top of our handclasp. She looked at my wedding ring.

"Your ring looks so much like my husband's wedding ring!"

I smiled slightly and changed the subject. "I can guarantee you one thing, Carole. I think your life is going to be wonderful."

I knew it was time to leave. I released our handshake. She thanked me and began to head back toward the glass double doors but suddenly stopped and strode back towards us as our backs were turned.

Without seeing her Doc, Louise and I moved to step onto Telluric Current One.

Just before we disappeared, I was surprised by feeling someone's hand on my forearm as we stepped onto our departure area. I turned. It was Carole.

The lowly, rumbling woosh of time and space enveloped *all* of us including her, interrupted only by one intense and yet breathy question, brushing past my cheek as she joined us.

"How did you know my name is Carole?"

Section XIV

Epilogue

While the years moved like Newtonian seconds for us, the other people of history spent decades forcing the United States Government to open its files on UFOs, UAPs and other neo-spiritual phenomena.

By 2060, the world was ready, willing and able to accept beings that moved inside and out of space, back and forth from universes. A sense of the public knowing that this was all 'true' provided an easy entrance of entities to planet Earth.

But the world was *not* ready for those entities that had come from a completely different *dimension* within planet Earth.

Leave it to Isaac Newton to point to the future. His discovered truth was more accurate now than when he lived on the Earth. And it became our mission to enlist his help as we moved towards the year 2060.

Epilogue

Special Thanks

To The White House Historical Association (https://www.whitehousehistory.org/) for the staff's help in my research of the Executive Mansion during the Lincoln Administration (1861-1865). As well, many thanks to WHHA President, Stewart McLaurin, for opening that era's door of the Executive Mansion for me.

To the late Stan Mattson, Founder and President Emeritus of the C.S. Lewis Foundation for his support and approval of including a fictional, yet accurate, inclusion of Jack Lewis' strength, dignity and creativity in this story. In many ways, *Empires of Dirt* is an homage to the work C. S. Lewis did in his own Space Trilogy – *Out of the Silent Planet, Perelandra* and *That Hideous Strength.* Those unfamiliar with these three books *must* acquire them. Many sincere thanks to my dear friend and in-law, Dave Bastedo, for opening that door a few years ago with Stan and the Foundation for the inclusion of Mr. Lewis in this tale of spacetime travel.

A special thanks to Barbara Wenda, Susan Mansfield and Shirley Silver for their work as editors of this book.

Works Consulted

Arnold, Kenneth; The Coming of the Saucers

Baier, Bret; To Rescue the Republic – Ulysses S. Grant – The Fragile Union and the Crisis of 1876

Buber-Neumann, Margarete; Under Two Dictators

Chesterton, G.K.; The Everlasting Man

Custer, Elizabeth; Boots and Saddles

Custer, George; My Life on the Plains

Danelek, J. Alan; Great Airship of 1897

Davis, Jefferson; The Rise and Fall of the Confederate Government Vol I & II

Du Bois, W.E.B.; Black Reconstruction in America 1860 – 1880

Eisenhower, Dwight D; In Review – Pictures I've Kept

Ellis, Shirley; Song lyrics to "The Name Game"

Ford, Pres. Gerald R; A Presidential Legacy and the Warren Commission

Freedman, Russell; Lincoln – A Photobiography

Graeber, David and Wengrow, David; The Dawn of Everything

Hamlin, Charles Eugene; The Life and Times of Hannibal Hamlin, Vol I & II

Hay, John M. & Nicolay, John G; Abraham Lincoln - A History Volumes I – X

Hitler, Adolf; Hitler's Second Book – The Unpublished Sequel to Mein Kampf

Jackson, Michael; Song lyrics to "Beat It"

Jacobs, Alan; The Narnian
Joel, William (Billy); Song lyrics to "It's Still Rock and Roll to Me"
Jones, Douglas C; The Court-Martial of George Armstrong Custer
Keel, John A.; Operation Trojan Horse
King, Sr, The Rev. Martin Luther; Daddy King – An Autobiography
King, Jr, The Rev. Martin Luther; The Autobiography of Martin Luther King, Jr.
King, Jr, The Rev. Martin Luther; The Papers of Martin Luther King, Jr.
Lewis, C. S.; Surprised by Joy
Lewis, C. S.; The Problem of Pain
Lewis, C. S.; The Screwtape Letters
Lewis, C. S.; The Space Trilogy: Out of the Silent Planet, Perelandra, That Hideous Strength
Lopach, James J, and Luckowski, Jean A; Jeannette Rankin; A Political Woman
Marquis, Thomas Bailey; Keep the Last Bullet for Yourself
McFadden, Phillip; The Man Who Walked with Giants
McLaren, Colin; JFK The Smoking Gun
Menninger, Bonar; Mortal Error – The Shot that Killed JFK
Metallica: https://blabbermouth.net/news/lars-ulrich-is-the-ringo-starr-of-heavy-metal-says-chris-jericho
Metallica: https://blackenedwhiskey.com/
Miller, David Humphreys; Custer's Fall: The Indian Side of the Story
Parr, Patrick; The Seminarian – Martin Luther King Jr. Comes of Age
Pickerell, Dave https://www.forbes.com/sites/fredminnick/2018/11/02/remembering-dave-pickerell-a-legendary-american-whiskey-distiller/?sh=6d2aaf266428
Randall, Ruth Painter; Mary Lincoln – Biography of a Marriage
Richardson, James D; Messages and Papers of the Presidents 1789–1897 Vol. VI 1861-1869
Roosevelt, Theodore; Theodore Roosevelt's Letters to his Children

Schroeder, Gerald L.; The Science of God – The Convergence of Scientific and Biblical Wisdom
Schwartz; C.S. Lewis on the Final Frontier
Scribner, Sons of Charles; Letters from Theodore Roosevelt to Anna Roosevelt Cowles 1870 - 1918
Stewart, Edgar; Custer's Luck
Sutton, Mathew Avery; American Apocalypse
Thorpe, Jim; History of the Olympics
Torres and LeMay; Early 20th Century UFOs
US Archives on UFOs and UAPs https://www.archives.gov/news/topics/ufos
Wheeler, Tom; Mr. Lincoln's T-Mails
Yankovic, Al; Song lyrics to "Eat It"

Printed in the United States
by Baker & Taylor Publisher Services

Printed in the United States
by Baker & Taylor Publisher Services